# Arthur Conan Doyle
# Sherlock Holmes
# and Devon

**Cover Illustration:**   The *Flag of Devon* inset with portrait photographs of Sir Arthur Conan Doyle, *Sir George Newnes, Dr George Turnavine Budd and Bertram Fletcher Robinson (from bottom left and clockwise respectively).

ii

# About the Authors

**Brian W. Pugh** is the Curator of The Conan Doyle (Crowborough) Establishment where he maintains the modest collection of Arthur Conan Doyle ephemera that is held by that organisation and their official website (http://www.the-conan-doyle-crowborough-establishment.com). He is the sole author of *A Chronology of the Life of Sir Arthur Conan Doyle* and also the joint author of *On the Trail of Arthur Conan Doyle* and *Bertram Fletcher Robinson*. Brian is a member of numerous Holmesian groups including The Sherlock Holmes Society of London. He lives at Lewes and is a retired former British Gas Engineering Supervisor.

**Paul R. Spiring** is a Chartered Biologist and Physicist. He is currently seconded by the British Government to work as the Head of Biology at the European School of Karlsruhe in Germany. Paul is also the joint author of *On the Trail of Arthur Conan Doyle* and *Bertram Fletcher Robinson* and has compiled a further four related books. He also maintains a tribute website that commemorates the memory of Bertram Fletcher Robinson (http://www.bfronline.biz) and is a member of the Devonshire Association and a number of Holmesian groups.

**Sadru Bhanji** is Vice-Chairman of the Devon and Exeter Institution and also Treasurer of the Exeter Branch of the Devonshire Association and past Treasurer of the Devon History Society. He is the author of *Barbary Pirates Off the Devon Coast* and *Postcards from Topsham*. Sadru has produced over thirty papers on Devon's local history for various journals including *The Lancet, Transactions of the Devonshire Association, The Devon Historian* and *Devon and Cornwall Notes and Queries*. He lives at Topsham near Exeter and is a retired Consultant Psychiatrist and University Lecturer.

**Frontispiece.** The Hound of the Baskervilles.
THE BRIAN PUGH COLLECTION.

*The Hound of the Baskervilles* by Arthur Conan Doyle was first serialised as nine monthly episodes within the British edition of *The Strand Magazine* (August 1901 – April 1902). This plate by Sidney Paget accompanied the first instalment of the story in that same periodical (Vol. XXII, No. 128, p. 122). It depicts the 'coal-black' spectral 'hell-hound' in hot pursuit of the 'wicked Hugo Baskerville' across Dartmoor in Devon.

# ARTHUR CONAN DOYLE

# SHERLOCK HOLMES

# AND DEVON

## A Complete Tour Guide & Companion

By

**Brian W. Pugh**

**Paul R. Spiring**

and

**Sadru Bhanji**

MX Publishing Limited
London

ISBN-13: 978-1904312864

Published by
MX Publishing Ltd.,
335 Princess Park Manor,
Royal Drive,
London,
N11 3GX.

www.mxpublishing.co.uk

Cover design by
Staunchdesign,
11 Shipton Road,
Woodstock,
Oxfordshire,
OX20 1LW.

www.staunch.com

# Dedication

Plate 1. A caricature of George Newnes by Leslie Ward.
It was published in *Vanity Fair* on 31 May 1894.

This book is dedicated to the memory of the British publisher
and politician, Sir George Newnes (13 March 1851 – 9 June
1910). He founded various periodicals including *The Strand
Magazine* in which many of the Sherlock Holmes stories were
first published. He was also pivotal to the development of the
twin towns of Lynton and Lynmouth in North Devon. During
1895, George Newnes was awarded the following hereditary
title: "1st Baronet, of Wildcroft, in the parish of Putney, in the
county of London; of Hollerday Hill, in the parish of Lynton,
and Hesketh House, in the borough of Torquay, both in the
county of Devon."

# Contents

# Chapter Three

## Sir George Newnes

# Chapter Four

## Bertram Fletcher Robinson

# Chapter Five

## The Arthur Conan Doyle, Sherlock Holmes & Devon Tour

# Foreword

This book is written by people who know their stuff. I have known Brian Pugh by reputation and through correspondence about Arthur Conan Doyle for many years and have appreciated the diligent work he has put into examining and documenting that person's life, particularly his chronology of events. The significant literary legacy of Bertram Fletcher Robinson would not be as widely known today without the efforts of Paul Spiring and I had the pleasure of dinner with him one night in late 2009 at which he broached the idea of my writing this Foreword – a proposal I was honoured to accept. I was unaware of Sadru Bhanji's work until being introduced to it via this book but for any research into the history of the Devon area his publications would be high on my list.

It is always good to pick up a book about the lives of interesting but disparate people that are intertwined in some way and to discover and explore the connecting links. In this case the central point is Arthur Conan Doyle and the three others, all absorbing characters in their own right, have their separate links to him. George Turnavine Budd, George Newnes and Bertram Fletcher Robinson all had a key part to play in Arthur Conan Doyle's character Sherlock Holmes achieving the popularity he has enjoyed ever since he first appeared in print 123 years ago and without a doubt will continue to enjoy for a very long time yet.

If George Turnavine Budd had had a more orthodox approach to treating people who came to him for a medical consultation and he and Conan Doyle had not subsequently fallen out then Conan Doyle may have had a steady and successful start to his medical career and not approached his writing of fiction with anywhere near the same level of necessity.

If George Newnes had not founded the immensely popular *Strand Magazine* at the time that Conan Doyle wrote his first two Sherlock Holmes short stories and then commissioned many more after their success then perhaps the Holmes adventures would have taken a lot longer to reach such a wide readership, if at all.

If Bertram Fletcher Robinson and Conan Doyle had not become such firm friends on the ship home from South Africa and thereafter Fletcher Robinson had fired up Conan Doyle's imagination with legendary tales of huge phantom dogs and the wilds of Dartmoor then maybe *The Hound of the Baskervilles* might not have been written, or have been written very differently.

This book contains a wealth of information – hard facts and interesting trivia – and displays considerable research and talent upon the part of the authors to present it so as to appeal to people across a broad spectrum. Anybody with the slightest interest in the history of Devon, the writings of Arthur Conan Doyle, the Sherlock Holmes phenomenon or the early days of popular publishing in Victorian and Edwardian times (the 'New Journalism') will find this book a highly interesting read and an indispensable reference. The expansive and comprehensive touring notes will take you to many interesting points and having this book in the car or backpack as you explore Devon will be like having the three authors along with you as knowledgeable tour guides.

Bill Barnes
'Captain' (president), The Sydney Passengers

# Preface

In November 1887, *Beeton's Christmas Annual* published a story entitled *A Study in Scarlet* that was written by a twenty-eight year old Southsea-based physician called Arthur Conan Doyle. It was the first of sixty stories that he wrote over forty years that each feature the now iconic literary detective, Mr Sherlock Holmes. This character has since appeared in around two-hundred and thirty films making him possibly the most filmed fictional character of all time.

The long-lasting appeal of Sherlock Holmes is due first and foremost to the story writing skills of his creator. However, there is little doubt that had it not been for three residents of Devon, the history of crime fiction might have been very different indeed. Firstly, George Turnavine Budd engineered the circumstances that prompted Conan Doyle to relocate to Southsea and spend more time at his writing-desk. Secondly, George Newnes delivered the Sherlock Holmes tales to a broad readership via the pages of the British and American editions of *The Strand Magazine*. Thirdly, Bertram Fletcher Robinson was pivotal to the inception of *The Hound of the Baskervilles*, which first appeared some eight years after Conan Doyle had 'slain' Holmes 'for good and all' in only his twenty-sixth adventure.

In this book, we scrutinise the impact that Budd, Newnes and Fletcher Robinson each brought to bear upon Arthur Conan Doyle's works. We also supply details about the ten visits that Conan Doyle paid to Devon between 1882 and 1923. We aim to engage all readers irrespective of their existing level of knowledge about the life and works of Arthur Conan Doyle. Furthermore, we hope that some interested individuals, groups and societies might use our book to help them retrace Conan Doyle's footsteps across Devon for themselves.

This book is in fact in two parts. The first four chapters will introduce the reader to the four major players, Sir Arthur Conan Doyle, Dr George Turnavine Budd, Sir George Newnes and Bertram Fletcher Robinson. The fifth chapter will enable the reader to partake in a real or virtual tour of the non-fictional sites in Devon that are associated with these major players.

The full *Arthur Conan Doyle, Sherlock Holmes and Devon Tour* incorporates thirty locations and fifty-six related points of interest. Visitors must drive one-hundred and fifty-five miles along various classifications of road and walk two miles along mainly flat footpaths. The full tour extends across West Devon, South Devon and North Devon and it encompasses Plymouth, Roborough, Princetown, Buckfastleigh, Ashburton, Newton Abbot, Ipplepen, Paignton, Torquay, Topsham, Exeter and Lynton respectively. Alternatively, readers may choose to reverse the suggested route or undertake one or more of the six localised sub-sections that comprise the full tour.

We would like to thank the following for their assistance with this book: Ann Adams (Budd family), Ashburton Library, Lesley & Roger Bacon (Budd family), Catriona Batty (Topsham Museum), Bill Barnes (President of The Sydney Passengers), Phillip G. Bergem (Norwegian Explorers), Michael Bourne (Baskerville family), Bob Brewis (Historian to Freemason Torbay Lodge No. 1358), Bristol Central Library, Bristol Record Office, Cambridge University Library, Graeme de Bracey Marrs (Robinson family), Patrick Casey (Clifton Rugby Club), Devon Record Office, Alistair Duncan (author), Shelah Duncan (The British Library), Simon Eliot (Headmaster of Sherborne School), Exeter Central Library, Michael Freeland (Harold Michelmore & Company Solicitors, Newton Abbot), Irene Ferguson (Edinburgh University), Arthur French (Ipplepen Archive), Laxmi Gadher (The National Archive, Richmond), General Register Office, John Genova, Stewart Gillies (The British Library), Annabel Gordon (TopFoto), Freda Howlett (President of The Sherlock Holmes Society of London), Ceri Hughes (Lynmouth & Lynton Lift Company), Roger Johnson (Editor of *The Sherlock Holmes Journal*), Tim Johnson (The Sherlock Holmes Collection, The University of Minnesota), Liverpool Central Library & Archive, Pat Luxford

(Ford Park Cemetery Trust), Lynton & Lynmouth Tourist Information Centre, Ian MacGregor (Met Office, Exeter), Janice McNabb, Newton Abbot Library, Fiona Muddeman (Cooke family), Peggy Perdue (The Friends of the Arthur Conan Doyle Collection, Toronto Public Library, Canada), Plymouth and West Devon Record Office, Plymouth Central Library, Mark Pool (Torquay Library), Charles Potter (Topsham Museum), Harry Rabbich, Christopher Redmond, John Richardson (Headmaster of Cheltenham College), Arthur Robinson (Robinson family), Mark Steed (Former Headmaster of Kelly College), Brian & Maggie Sutton, Troy Taylor (The Illinois Hauntings Tour Company), The Devon and Exeter Institution, The Trustees of Topsham Museum, Philip Weller (The Baskerville Hounds, The Dartmoor Sherlock Holmes Study Group and The Conan Doyle Study Group), Frances Willmoth (Jesus College, Cambridge University), Doug Wrigglesworth (The Friends of the Arthur Conan Doyle Collection, Toronto Public Library, Canada).

Finally, we would like to extend a special thank you to Dr. John Travis for giving us his permission to reproduce pictures from his two books; *An Illustrated History of Lynton and Lynmouth, 1770-1914* (1995) and *Lynton and Lynmouth: Glimpses of the Past* (1997). Both of these works proved to be invaluable to us in the preparation of Chapter 3 and it is our opinion that he has done more than anyone else to record the history of both Lynton and Lynmouth. Interested readers will locate further details about Dr. Travis' books in the *Further Reading* section at the rear of this book.

The game is afoot.
Happy touring!


Brian W. Pugh,
Paul R. Spiring
& Sadru Bhanji.

Devon,
June 2010.

# CHAPTER ONE

# Sir Arthur Conan Doyle
## (22 May 1859 – 7 July 1930)

Plate 2.  Sir Arthur Conan Doyle.
THE BRIAN PUGH COLLECTION.

# Introduction

Arthur Ignatius Conan Doyle (hereinafter ACD) was born on 22 May 1859 at 11 Picardy Place in Edinburgh (see Plate 2). He was the eldest son of an artist and architect called Charles Altamont Doyle and Mary Josephine Doyle (née Foley). ACD was baptised into the Roman Catholic religion and given the name Conan in order to perpetuate the name of his childless godfather and great uncle, Michael Conan. ACD was one of nine children and his siblings were as follows: Annette (22 July 1856 – 13 January 1890), Catherine (22 April 1858 – 20 October 1858), Mary (4 May 1861 – 3 June 1863) Caroline (22 February 1866 – 3 May 1941), Constance (4 March 1868 – 8 June 1924), John (31 March 1873 – 19 February 1919), Jane (16 March 1875 – 1 July 1937) and Bryan Mary (16 March 1877 – 8 February 1927).

ACD was initially educated at the Newington Academy in Edinburgh. At the age of eight years he was sent to a Jesuit preparatory school called Hodder in Lancashire. Two years later, he was admitted to nearby Stonyhurst College. At the age of sixteen, ACD left Stonyhurst and continued his education for one year at a sister school called Stella Matutina at Feldkirch in Austria. During his return home to Scotland, ACD stopped-over in Paris to spend some weeks with Michael Conan, who urged him to consider a medical career. Upon his arrival in Edinburgh, ACD learned that it had in fact been predetermined that he would study medicine and not the arts as he himself had hoped. This decision was probably influenced by a family friend and physician called Dr Bryan Charles Waller who boarded with the Doyle family at this time.

# The Early Medical Years

It has been widely reported that ACD entered Edinburgh University Medical School during October 1876 (Waller's Alma Mater). However, a note written on 17 May 1882 by one Thomas Gilbert, the then 'Clerk to Edinburgh University', states that ACD actually began his medical studies there on 1 November 1877. In any event, during his time as a student, ACD was taught by Dr Joseph Bell, upon whom the character Sherlock Holmes was largely based. He also met Professor William Rutherford, who was a model for a later fictional character called Professor George Edward Challenger.

During June 1879, ACD began working as a medical assistant to one Dr Reginald Hoare in Birmingham. In October of that same year, ACD returned to Edinburgh and was befriended by a final-year medical student called George Turnavine Budd. During January 1880, he attended a lecture in Birmingham that was entitled *Does Death End All?* He professed to having found the subject interesting but unconvincing. Nevertheless, ACD maintained a life-long interest in psychical phenomenon from thereon in.

During February 1880, ACD started working as an unqualified surgeon aboard a whaling ship called *Hope* that was destined for the Arctic Circle. He was paid a flat rate of two pounds and ten shillings per month, plus an additional three shillings for every ton of whale oil that was collected. During this voyage, ACD fell from the ice into the freezing sea and narrowly escaped from drowning by using a skinned seal carcass to pull himself out. On 10 August of that same year, ACD returned to Scotland and thereafter rejoined Dr Hoare in Birmingham.

On 1 August 1881, ACD was awarded both a first class Bachelors degree in Medicine and a Masters degree in Surgery from Edinburgh University. In October of that same year, he was employed as a surgeon aboard a cargo steamer called *Mayumba* that was bound for West Africa. During this trip he contracted typhoid and almost died. In January 1882, ACD returned to England and thereafter rejoined Dr Hoare in Birmingham for a third and final time. In early May of that same year, he became a junior medical partner to George Turnavine Budd in the East Stonehouse district of what is now the city of Plymouth in Devon (see Chapter 2).

During June 1882, ACD travelled to Tavistock from East Stonehouse and he stopped on-route at Roborough. This excursion inspired him to write an article entitled *Dry Plates on a Wet Moor* that was published in *The British Journal of Photography* in November 1882. The 'genius' referred to in that article is probably George Turnavine Budd, who also appears very thinly disguised in a short story entitled *Crabbe's Practice* (1884). In 1892, ACD wrote a Sherlock Holmes story entitled *The Adventure of Silver Blaze* that is set about Tavistock. Later, ACD used Budd as the model for a character called 'Dr James Cullingworth' in two books entitled *The Stark Munro Letters* (1895) and *Memories and Adventures* (1924).

In late June 1882, the partnership between Dr George Turnavine Budd and ACD was dissolved. Hence, ACD decided to leave Plymouth for Portsmouth in Hampshire armed with only £10 in his pocket and a 'devil-may-care optimism of youth as to the future'. He then rented a house at 1 Bush Villas, Elm Grove, Southsea and also set up a medical practice there (see Plate 3). However, business was slow at first and he later recalled that there 'was a grocer who developed epileptic fits, which meant butter and tea for me'. Nevertheless, over the eight years that ACD worked in Southsea, he became a reasonably successful physician and earned as much as £300 a year.

During early 1885, ACD treated a twenty-five year old patient called John Hawkins, who was affectionately referred to as 'Jack' by his family. John was suffering from the then incurable disease of bacterial meningitis. He was taken to see ACD by his twenty-seven year old sister, Louisa Hawkins. At that time, meningitis sufferers were frequently ostracised by society because the cause of their alarming convulsions was not known.

Nevertheless, ACD installed John in his home and nursed him prior to his death on 25 March 1885.

Plate 3. ACD at Southsea (circa 1888).
THE BRIAN PUGH COLLECTION.

Plate 4. 'Louise' Hawkins ('Touie').
THE TROY TAYLOR COLLECTION.

Louisa Hawkins (10 April 1857 – 4 July 1906) preferred to be addressed as 'Louise' and for that reason, she was nicknamed

'Touie' (see Plate 4). Louise was 'a very feminine home-loving girl of great gentleness and complete unselfishness'. ACD and Louise married on 6 August 1885, just five days after he was awarded a Doctorate of Medicine by Edinburgh University. The wedding was held at Thornton-in-Lonsdale in Yorkshire and Dr Bryan Charles Waller acted as ACD's best man. Later, ACD wrote of Louise that 'no man could have had a more gentle and amiable life's companion'.

During 1886, ACD wrote *A Study in Scarlet* in which he introduced his legendary detective, Sherlock Holmes. This story was first published during 1887 in *Beeton's Christmas Annual* and it was later republished as a book by Ward, Lock & Company Limited of London (1888). Originally ACD intended to entitle this story *A Tangled Skein* and use two principal characters called 'Sherrinford Holmes' and 'Ormond Sacker'. However, feeling these names to be somewhat awkward, he changed them to Sherlock Holmes and Dr John Watson. The character of Watson probably derived his name from one Dr James Watson, who was present when ACD was initiated as a Freemason at Portsmouth Lodge No. 257 on 26 January 1887.

On 28 January 1889, Louise gave birth to their first child, a daughter called Mary Louise Conan Doyle (d. 12 June 1976). On 30 August of that same year, ACD attended a literary soirée at the world-famous Langham Hotel in London. It was hosted by the American editor, Joseph Marshall Stoddart (1845-1921), who wished to recruit British writers for his Philadelphia-based literary magazine, *Lippincott's*. As a direct result, ACD wrote a second Sherlock Holmes long story entitled, *The Sign of Four* (1890). That same dinner also prompted Oscar Wilde to write his only novel, *The Picture of Dorian Grey* (1890).

In 1891, ACD left Southsea and travelled to Vienna with the intention of studying eye medicine. However, this plan fell through and he relocated to London and opened his own surgery instead. Business was slow, so ACD soon abandoned medicine altogether in favour of writing.

# Beyond All Medical Help!

During January 1891, George Newnes launched *The Strand Magazine*. Previously, he had also founded *The Westminster Gazette* (1873), *Tit-Bits* (1881), *The Wide World Magazine* (1888) and *Review of Reviews* (1890). The first twenty-four Sherlock Holmes short stories were each published in *The Strand Magazine* between July 1891 and December 1893. The remaining thirty-two Sherlock Holmes short stories were first published between August 1901 and March 1927 in *The Strand Magazine* (15), *Collier's Weekly Magazine* (11) and *Liberty* (6). Clearly, George Newnes was pivotal in delivering Sherlock Holmes to a global audience and his links with both ACD and Devon are further explored in Chapter 3 of this book.

During July 1891, *The Strand Magazine* published a Sherlock Holmes adventure entitled *A Scandal in Bohemia*. This proved to be so successful that ACD was commissioned to write a further eleven Sherlock Holmes short stories that were each published in *The Strand Magazine* between August 1891 and June 1892. In October 1892, all twelve of these stories were republished in a book entitled *The Adventures of Sherlock Holmes* (London: George Newnes Ltd.). Each of these stories was illustrated by an artist called Sidney Paget and ACD was paid between £35 and £50 per story. However by November 1891, ACD was weary of Sherlock Holmes and remarked in a letter to his mother that he was considering 'slaying Holmes in the last and winding him up for good and all'.

During February 1892, ACD accepted an offer of £1000 to write a second series of Sherlock Holmes stories for *The Strand Magazine*. Later that same year, ACD travelled with his family to Norway where he skied for the first time. On 15 November 1892, Louise gave birth to a second healthy child called Arthur Alleyne Kingsley Conan Doyle (affectionately referred to as 'Kingsley'). He was baptised on 22 December at St. Mary's Church, South Norwood, London (d. 28 October 1918).

On 16 December 1892, ACD attended a dinner at the Reform Club in Pall Mall. This dinner was held to celebrate the pending publication of the one-hundredth edition of a Cambridge University undergraduate periodical entitled *The Granta*. ACD sat next to a fellow Reformer called John Robinson who managed *The Daily News* and was an uncle of Bertram Fletcher Robinson (see Chapter 4). Both men were friends of a fellow guest and club member called Thomas Wemyss Reid who had previously edited the *Leeds Mercury*. This newspaper is referred to by Sherlock Holmes in Chapter IV of *The Hound of the Baskervilles*.

In around August 1893, ACD and Louise spent some time at Lucerne in Switzerland. During this trip the couple visited the Reichenbach Falls near Meiringen. Shortly after their return to England, Louise was diagnosed with tuberculosis and given just a few months to live. ACD responded to this bleak prognosis by taking Louise to Davos in Switzerland where it was hoped that the climate might relieve her symptoms.

In December 1893, Sherlock Holmes was "killed-off" at the Reichenbach Falls in a story entitled *The Adventure of the Final Problem*. This was the twenty-sixth Sherlock Holmes adventure and it concluded the second series of twelve short stories that were each first published within *The Strand Magazine*. Shortly thereafter the second series of short stories was compiled and republished in a book entitled *The Memoirs of Sherlock Holmes* (London: George Newnes Ltd.).

Between 2 October and 8 December 1894, ACD toured North America with his younger brother, John Francis Innes Hay Doyle (see Plate 5). On 3 November 1894, ACD wrote to John Robinson from Amherst House, Amherst in Massachusetts. Robinson had recently been knighted and elected to the committee of the Reform Club. In his letter ACD discussed the first five weeks of his first North America lecture-tour and he also detailed the arrangements for his return to England. He began this letter thus:

MY DEAR ROBINSON

May I make you my mouth-piece in conveying my
warm remembrances to friends of the Reform, above
all to Payn and Reid?

ACD seldom addressed his friends by their Christian names; the
same formal greeting was later used in two acknowledgements
that were published in the first book editions of *The Hound of
the Baskervilles* (see Chapter 4).

On 15 December 1894, ACD returned to England from
America. Four months later, *The Strand Magazine* published
the first in a series of short stories by ACD that featured a new
hero called Brigadier Etienne Gerard.

During 1895, the author Grant Allen suggested to ACD that the
air in Surrey might be beneficial to the health of Louise. ACD
subsequently purchased a plot of land in Hindhead and
commissioned his architect friend, Joseph Henry Ball, to design
a house. It was built by October 1897 and named Undershaw.

Throughout the summer of 1895, ACD and Louise holidayed in
Switzerland. In January 1896, ACD had the first of a twelve-
part serialisation entitled *Rodney Stone* published in *The Strand
Magazine*. That same month, ACD and Louise embarked upon
a Nile cruise between Egypt and Sudan. During this trip, brief
hostilities broke out between the British and Dervishes and
ACD acted as a war correspondent for *The Westminster Gazette*.
This experience inspired his dramatic desert story *The Tragedy
of the Korosko* that was first published in *The Strand Magazine*
between May and December 1897. In April 1896, ACD and
Louise returned to Hindhead but Undershaw was not completed.
Hence, they decided to rent a nearby property called Grayswood
Beeches.

# The 'Innes' & Outs of Love

On 1 February 1897, ACD travelled to Devon to meet the family of a woman that had caught the eye of his twenty-three year old brother 'Innes' Doyle (see Plate 5). Innes was a commissioned officer with the Western Division of the Royal Artillery and was stationed at Higher Barracks in Exeter. The girl in question was Dora Geraldine Hamilton (1877 – 1950). She resided with her parents and a large staff of servants at a mansion house called The Retreat in Topsham (now a suburb of Exeter). Dora was the daughter of Alexander Kelso Hamilton (1854 – 1929) and Caroline Hamilton née Porter (1855 – 1906). Alexander and 'Lina' married in 1876 and they had one other daughter called Rose Vera Hamilton who died during her early childhood (1884 – 1890). The day before ACD left Hindhead to visit Innes in Devon he wrote the following related comments in a letter that was sent to his mother:

> I go down tomorrow to see Innes at Exeter and I shall return on Friday when I am to be present at the Nansen [a Norwegian Arctic explorer] reception in London. I am really going down west because I thought it well to know the Hamiltons as Innes seemed to have some designs upon Miss Dora. It may all be nothing but it can do no harm that I should be on terms with her people. They give a dance on Tuesday. She is an only child – lots of money – 20.16 hands (Beg pardon, just been buying a horse).

Alexander Kelso Hamilton (see Plate 6) was a prominent local landowner and he played a large part in both the affairs of Topsham and Devon. Somewhat old-fashioned in his ways, he refused to own a motor car and would often be seen driving around Topsham in his horse-drawn carriage well into the Twentieth Century. Hamilton was a keen sailor and a founding member of Topsham Sailing Club. He also possessed several boats including one named *Dora*. In February 1898, Dora Hamilton married a Royal Artillery officer called Major Arthur

William B. Gordon at St. Margaret's Church in Topsham. The couple later had two children, a daughter named Phoebe Gordon (b. 1904) and a son called Kelso Gordon (b. 1909). Major Gordon was the son of the eminently respectable Major-General Gordon of Titchfield in Hampshire.

It is not known whether Dora was aware of Innes' feelings towards her. In any event, it is unlikely that her father would have approved of Innes for several reasons. Firstly, Alexander Hamilton was a staunch Protestant whilst Innes was raised as a Roman Catholic. Secondly, Alexander Hamilton was a prominent member of Victorian High-Society whilst Innes' father, Charles Altamont Doyle had died as an 'inmate' of a Scottish mental asylum during 1893. Happily, Innes did eventually find true love and happiness in the form of a Danish woman called Clara Claudia Schwensen (29 March 1881 – 3 November 1930). The couple were married in Copenhagen on 2 August 1911 and thereafter they had two sons, John Reinhold Innes (24 June 1913 – 2 May 1987) and Francis Kingsley (1 November 1917 – 29/30 May 1942).

Plate 5. Colonel John Francis Innes Hay Doyle
THE BRIAN PUGH COLLECTION.

11

Plate 6.  Alexander Kelso Hamilton (circa 1915).

## 'Arise, Sir Arthur!'

On 15 March 1897, thirty-seven year old ACD attended a party in London and met a woman called Jean Leckie who was to become his second wife (see Plate 7).  Jean (14 March 1874 – 27 June 1940) was the twenty-three year old daughter of a Scottish family who were then living at Blackheath in Kent. She was well-read, a skilled horsewoman and a trained opera singer.  It was a genuine love-match but ACD continued to nurse and cherish Louise until her death in 1906.  ACD's family and friends were naturally divided upon the subject of Jean Leckie but some accepted her into their circle.

12

Plate 7. Jean Leckie (1907).

During October 1899, The Second Boer War (1899 – 1902) began in South Africa. Shortly thereafter, ACD tried to enlist with the Middlesex Yeomanry but the military authorities rejected him because of his age and general condition. In spite of this set-back, during late February 1900, ACD sailed to South Africa in order to take up a voluntary position as a physician at the Langman Hospital in Bloemfontein. During his service there, he contracted dysentery and also experienced a recurrence of typhoid fever. In July of that same year, a weakened ACD returned to England in the company of Bertram Fletcher Robinson aboard the *SS Briton* (see Chapter 4).

During the summer of 1900, ACD played for Marylebone Cricket Club (M.C.C.) against London County at Crystal Palace in London. During this game he recorded his only first-class wicket by dismissing the famous Bristol-born cricketer, Dr William Gilbert 'WG' Grace (then aged 52 years).

In October 1900, ACD was defeated as the Conservative and Liberal Unionist parliamentary candidate for Edinburgh Central. Later that same month, Smith, Elder & Company published *The Great Boer War,* a book that ACD constantly updated. When the war concluded in 1902, this book had run to at least sixteen editions.

On 31 March 1901, Louise and her mother, Emily Hawkins, stayed at Bolton's Boarding House, Tor Church Road, Torquay, Devon. Meanwhile, ACD was staying with his mother and Jean Leckie at the Ashdown Forest Hotel in Forest Row near East Grinstead in Sussex. ACD's two children, twelve year old Mary and eight year old 'Kingsley', remained at Undershaw in the care of their spinster aunt who was also called Emily Hawkins.

On 26 April 1901, ACD and Bertram Fletcher Robinson took a three day golfing holiday at the Royal Links Hotel in Cromer, Norfolk. Four weeks later, the two men visited Dartmoor together and they stayed at the Duchy Hotel in Princetown. By September 1901, ACD had written *The Hound of the Baskervilles,* thereby 'resurrecting' Sherlock Holmes. This largely Devon-based story has since formed the basis of the plot for at least twenty-four theatrical films and many television adaptations.

On 16 January 1902, ACD's views about The Second Boer War were published in a sixpenny pamphlet entitled *The War in South Africa – Its Cause and Conduct.* This work was probably prompted by public unease over foreign reports of alleged British atrocities and the use of concentration camps. ACD did not condone the conditions in such camps, but he argued that there was a need to isolate guerrilla Boers from the homestead families that supported their activities. Such defence of British policy in layman terms won him unprecedented public acclaim. The pamphlet was translated into numerous languages and it sold in record numbers; ACD donated the revenue that was generated from the sale of his pamphlet to various good causes, which included a reconciliation fund for disadvantaged Boers. The Second Boer War ended during May of that same year with the signing of the Treaty of Vereeniging.

In around August 1902, ACD secured a job for twenty year old Robert Leckie, the youngest brother of Jean Leckie, at George Newnes' office. That same month, he played several cricket matches at Teignmouth in South Devon. About that same time, Jean Leckie and her mother, Selina Leckie, travelled to Teignmouth from North Devon where they had been holidaying. On 16 August 1902, ACD wrote to his mother and stated that he intended to meet Jean at Newton Abbot on 23 August. He added that they would drive 'over some of the Baskerville Moor Country' and that 'it will be charming'. Thereafter ACD also met Jean in nearby Exeter and they visited Higher Barracks where Innes was stationed in 1897. During early September 1902, ACD travelled to Lynton in North Devon and delivered a speech to mark the unveiling of a bust to George Newnes (see page 63).

On 24 October 1902, ACD went to Buckingham Palace where he was both knighted and appointed a Deputy Lieutenant of Surrey by King Edward VII. Officially, he was honoured for services to his country during The Second Boer War. However, it is worth noting that Edward VII was an avid Sherlock Holmes fan and that he had attended the gala performance of William Gillette's play entitled *Sherlock Holmes* at *The Lyceum Theatre* on 1 February 1902.

In 1903, ACD travelled to Birmingham and purchased a ten-horse power Wolseley motorcar. After very little training in its operation, he then elected to drive one-hundred and fifty miles back to Undershaw. That same year also marked the publication of a second series of the *Brigadier Gerard* stories. ACD was then persuaded to continue the revival of Sherlock Holmes and subsequently wrote a further thirteen short stories that appeared in *The Strand Magazine* between October 1903 and December 1904 (illustrated by Sidney Paget). In 1905, these stories were compiled and published as *The Return of Sherlock Holmes* by George Newnes Limited.

In early 1904, ACD was invited to join a select twelve man London-based crime club called 'Our Society'. Bertram Fletcher Robinson and Max Pemberton were also elected at the same time (see Chapter 4). On 18 June of that same year, both ACD and Bertram Fletcher Robinson attended a dinner at the Savoy Hotel in London that was held to honour Lord Roberts. This dinner was hosted by Joseph Hodges Choate, the then American Ambassador to the United Kingdom. The guest list included many British dignitaries, all of whom were members of an Anglo-American society entitled 'The Pilgrims'.

On 7 April 1905, ACD was awarded the honorary degree of Doctorate of Letters by Edinburgh University. Later that same month, he visited the sites of the notorious Whitechapel Murders committed by 'Jack the Ripper'. He was accompanied by Dr Samuel Ingleby Oddie (later His Majesty's Coroner for Central London) and several other members of 'Our Society'.

During January 1906, ACD was defeated as the Unionist parliamentary candidate for the Hawick Division of the Scottish Borders. In the early hours of 4 July of that same year, the first Lady Conan Doyle died aged forty-nine years. She was buried in Grayshot Churchyard near the family home at Hindhead in Surrey. Understandably, ACD was deeply affected by her death and he entered into a deep depression.

In August 1906, ACD visited the Leckie family home called Monkstown at Lordswell Lane in Crowborough (Sussex). His friendship with Jean Leckie now blossomed and they were soon to become engaged. Just down the lane from Monkstown was a cottage called Little Windlesham that was owned by a Mrs Scott-Malden. ACD fell in love with this house, purchased it, enlarged it and then renamed it Windlesham.

# A Second Family and Other Interests

In around January 1907, ACD began actively campaigning for a free pardon for George Edalji who was convicted of cattle maiming during 1903. Consequently, ACD made frequent trips between Undershaw and London to visit the Home Office, Scotland Yard and the offices of *The Daily Telegraph*. Edalji was eventually released during May 1907.

On 18 September 1907, ACD married Jean Leckie at St. Margaret's Church, Westminster, London. The reception was held at The Whitehall Rooms at the Hôtel Métropole and it was attended by amongst others, Max Pemberton, Jerome K. Jerome, Bram Stoker, J.M. Barrie, Sir George Newnes and George Edalji. During their honeymoon, ACD received 'The Order of the Second Class of the Medjideh' from Sultan Abdul-Hamid in Constantinople, the then capital of the Ottoman Empire. In late 1907, the newly-weds moved into Windlesham at Hurtis Hill in Crowborough. It was here in his study (see Plate 8) that ACD wrote many of his most enduring books: *Round the Fire Stories* (1908), *The Lost World* (1912), *The Poison Belt* (1913), *The Valley of Fear* (1915), *His Last Bow* (1917), *The British Campaign in France and Flanders* (1916 – 1920), *Tales of Adventure and Medical Life* (1922), *Memories and Adventures* (1924), *The Land of Mist* (1926), *The Casebook of Sherlock Holmes* (1927) and *The Maracot Deep and Other Stories* (1929).

During 1908, ACD was employed by *The Daily Mail* newspaper to report upon the Olympic Games that were being staged at White City Stadium in London. During this event, he witnessed the disqualification of an Italian marathon runner called Dorando Pietri for receiving medical attention and a helping hand shortly before crossing the finishing line in first place. Queen Alexandra presented Dorando with a gold cup in recognition of his efforts and ACD subsequently presented him with a cheque for £308 and a gold cigarette case.

Plate 8. ACD at Windlesham.

In January 1909, ACD fell seriously ill with an intestinal blockage and underwent an operation at Windlesham. On 17 March of that same year, Jean gave birth to their first son called Denis Stewart Percy Conan Doyle (d. 9 March 1955). During the summer, ACD assisted a Torquay-born nurse called Joan Paynter, to ascertain the whereabouts of her missing Danish fiancé. ACD was able to reveal to her both where the man had gone and how undeserving this sailor was of her affections!

On the evening of 18 November 1909, ACD delivered a lecture entitled *The Congo Atrocity* at the Plymouth Guildhall. He was part of a deputation from the Congo Reform Association that sought to publicise the recent ill treatment of the Congolese population by King Leopold II of Belgium. ACD was accompanied by a founder member of the C.R.A. called Edmund Dene Morel, who was a British journalist, author and socialist politician. The meeting was called at the behest of John Yeo, the then Mayor of Plymouth and he presided over the proceedings. It was well attended and ACD's talk was warmly received. Following a vote of thanks that was proposed by the then Mayor of Devonport, William Littleton, ACD stated that he felt that the Westcountry firmly backed the Congolese cause.

Between 7 and 21 March 1910, ACD and Jean spent a two-week holiday in Cornwall and they stayed at the Poldhu Hotel in Mullion near Helston. Shortly after this visit, ACD wrote a Cornwall-based Sherlock Holmes adventure entitled *The Devil's Foot*. This story was first published in *The Strand Magazine* during December 1910.

In April 1910, ACD became interested in the case of Oscar Slater, a German Jew, who was accused of committing a murder in Scotland. Slater was originally sentenced to hang but he was reprieved and sentenced to life imprisonment during 1909 instead. Thanks partially to the efforts of ACD, Slater was released from prison in 1927 and his sentence was quashed in 1928.

During 1910, ACD was appointed as the captain of an M.C.C. team that participated in several successive annual cricket tours of Devon. ACD also recalled that during these tours, he played various local teams including Plymouth, Exeter and Devonshire. In October 1910, he was also elected captain of Crowborough Golf Club and president of Crowborough Gymnasium Club. On 19 November of that same year, Jean gave birth to a second son called Adrian Malcolm Conan Doyle (d. 3 June 1970).

In 1911, Lady Conan Doyle was made captain of the ladies' section of Crowborough Golf Club. Jean was probably, like most other lady captains, a non-playing member. That same summer, ACD drove a Dietrich-Lorraine car in the Prince Henry's Tour (an Anglo-German motor race that was won by the British). On 2 August 1911, ACD's brother Innes married a Danish girl called Clara Schwensen in Copenhagen. Towards the end of that year, ACD spoke of finding a fossil footprint near Windlesham. A cast of a similar footprint can still be viewed in the Tunbridge Wells Museum in Kent.

During 1912, ACD introduced a character called Professor George Edward Challenger in an eight-part serialisation entitled *The Lost World* that first appeared in *The Strand Magazine* (April – November). A silent version of this story was the first film to be screened on an aeroplane during a flight that departed from Croydon Aerodrome on 7 April 1925. In August 1912, ACD was placed in charge of the British Olympic Committee ahead of the 1916 Berlin Games that was subsequently cancelled due to the onset of the WWI. On 21 December 1912, Jean gave birth to a daughter called Jean Lena Annette Conan Doyle (later Air Commandant Dame Jean Conan Doyle, Lady Bromet). All five of ACD's children died childless and his direct line of descent was ended upon the death of Dame Jean on 18 November 1997.

In March 1913, ACD campaigned for a channel tunnel link between England and France (it was to be another eighty-one years before such a link was constructed). He also organised a gold hunt on Crowborough golf links course for six half-sovereigns. The following month, ACD made a speech to the National League for Opposing Woman Suffrage at Tunbridge Wells. Thereafter acid was poured through a letter pillar-box outside Windlesham by suffragettes; a police constable was subsequently stationed to guard the gate to ACD's home.

During 1914, ACD was invited to open the drill hall of the 'G2 Crowborough Company of the 5th Battalion Royal Sussex Regiment'. He then embarked upon a two-month tour of North America. Upon his return, WWI began and he formed a volunteer local home guard unit. This body was later replaced by the official '4th Volunteer Battalion of the Royal Sussex', in which ACD served as a private.

In March 1915, ACD and Lady Jean took a two-week holiday in Torquay and they stayed at The Grand Hotel. On the afternoon of 27 March, ACD gave an illustrated lecture entitled *The Great Battles of the War* at The Pavilion on the seafront. This meeting was presided over by the local Member of Parliament, Colonel Charles Rosdew Burn. During his talk, ACD described the events that precipitated WWI and culminated in the First Battle of Ypres (19 October 1914 – 22 November 1914). He also paid 'high tribute' to the Devonshire Regiment and urged young men to give their strength 'the rich man his money, the workman his labour, and the women their husbands and sons.'

After the Dublin Easter Rising of 1916, ACD campaigned for the reprieve of Sir Roger Casement, a founder member of the Congo Reform Association, who was convicted of treason. On this occasion, his intervention failed and Casement was hanged at Pentonville Prison. Later that same year, ACD announced his full conversion to Spiritualism in an article that was published in a psychic magazine named *Light*. Thereafter ACD wrote that the 'subject of psychical research is one upon which I have thought more and about which I have been slower to form my opinion, than upon any other subject whatsoever.'

On 28 October 1918, ACD's eldest son, Captain Arthur Alleyne Kingsley Conan Doyle, died from post-war pneumonia, having been weakened by wounds that he received during the Battle of the Somme. Barely four months later, ACD's beloved brother 'acting Brigadier-General' John Francis Innes Hay Doyle, also died after falling victim to the post-war influenza epidemic.

## The Twilight Years

On the afternoon of 4 August 1920, ACD gave a lecture entitled *Death and the Hereafter* at Exeter Hippodrome. This meeting was presided over by F. T. Blake, the then President of the Southern Counties Union of Spiritualists. The next evening he delivered the same lecture at Torquay Town Hall to an audience that largely comprised of women. On this occasion the meeting was presided over by one Henry Paul Rabbich, the then President of Paignton Spiritualist Society and Vice-President of the Southern Counties Union of Spiritualists. Later, ACD recalled that the Town Hall 'was next to a church, and just as I started to speak the church bells began ringing, and I had to shout all the time.' During this visit, ACD stayed with Rabbich at his home called The Kraal that is situated at 5 Headland Grove, Preston, Paignton (see page 167). Rabbich was also a prominent local builder and Freemason at Torbay Lodge No. 1358.

On 13 August 1920, ACD commenced a voyage to Australia and New Zealand to deliver a series of public lectures about Spiritualism. During this tour, ACD learnt of the death of his eighty-three year old mother, Mary Doyle (8 July 1837 – 30 December 1920). Over the course of the following three years, ACD also lectured on Spiritualism in Great Britain, France and North America.

On 20 February 1923, ACD and his wife returned to Devon for the last time. They resided at the Victoria Hotel, Belgrave Road, Torquay. The following evening ACD delivered a lecture entitled *The New Revelation* at The Pavilion. This meeting was presided over by G.H. Tredale, the then Mayor of Torquay. On 22 February 1923, ACD and his wife travelled to Plymouth and they stayed at the Grand Hotel. The next evening ACD delivered the same lecture to an audience at Plymouth Guildhall. This meeting was presided over by one W.H. Watkins on behalf of Solomon Stephens, the then Mayor of Plymouth. It is worth noting that the Grand Hotel was located next to Elliot Terrace where ACD had lived with George Turnavine Budd during 1882. This might explain why he wrote about Budd in his autobiography, *Memories and Adventures*, which was first serialised in *The Strand Magazine* between October 1923 and July 1924.

During 1924, ACD became interested in the case of the so-called 'chicken run murder'. This crime was committed at Blackness in Crowborough and one Norman Thorne was subsequently convicted. ACD felt that this judgement was largely based upon circumstantial evidence and was therefore unsafe. He raised these concerns in letters to the press, but to no avail. Thorne was hanged at Wandsworth Prison on 22 April 1925.

Between October 1921 and April 1927, the final twelve Sherlock Holmes tales were first published in *The Strand Magazine* (4), *Collier's Weekly Magazine* (2) and *Liberty* (6). They were then compiled and republished as *The Case-Book of Sherlock Holmes* by John Murray in June 1927. It is generally agreed that this final collection of stories was the weakest of all the Holmes adventures.

During the winter of 1928, ACD began a tour of several African nations in order to promote Spiritualism. He returned to England during the spring of 1929, having also visited both Egypt and Malta. Just six months later, ACD delivered a series of lectures about Spiritualism in the Netherlands, Denmark, Sweden and Norway. He returned home exhausted and thereafter suffered a heart attack. ACD rallied a little during the spring of 1930 but then collapsed once again and resigned himself to the prospect of death, which of course, he perceived as a new beginning and not as an end. Indeed, ACD remarked in a letter: 'I wait with a mind which is full of contentment, I have had many adventures. The greatest and most glorious awaits me now.'

Despite his declining health, on 1 July 1930, ACD led a deputation to the British Home Secretary, John Robert Clynes, to promote the cause of Spiritualism. Just six days later, ACD suffered a fatal heart attack in his bedroom next to his first floor study at Windlesham. At his request, he was propped in a chair, looking out towards Crowborough Common and Golf Course. His sons, Denis and Adrian, had raced off to Tunbridge Wells to fetch oxygen that was unobtainable in Crowborough at the time. Nevertheless, at 08.17 on Monday 7 July 1930, ACD died surrounded by many members of his family.

On 11 July 1930 following a short funeral service, ACD was buried within the grounds of Windlesham. The original grave marker was made of British oak and the inscription read 'Blade Straight, Steel True'. ACD's grave was located next to his writing hut under a copper beech. Many local and national dignitaries attended both the funeral service and the subsequent memorial service that was also held at the Albert Hall in London on 13 July.

Lady Jean Conan Doyle continued to live at Windlesham until her death on 27 June 1940 aged sixty-six years. She was buried beside ACD's grave. On the sale of the Windlesham estate in 1955, the two bodies were exhumed and then re-buried together within the graveyard of All Saints Church, Minstead, Hampshire (see Plate 9). The inscription on the new gravestone was altered to read 'Steel True, Blade Straight'.

Plate 9. The grave of ACD and
the Second Lady Conan Doyle.
THE BRIAN PUGH COLLECTION.

# CHAPTER TWO

## Dr George Turnavine Budd
### (3 November 1855 – 28 February 1889)

Plate 10.  Dr George Turnavine Budd (circa 1882).
COURTESY OF MACDONALD & JANE'S (LONDON).

# Introduction

Dr George Turnavine Budd (hereinafter GTB) was an extremely charismatic personality (see Plate 10). During the 1880s, he became a well-known physician in the East Stonehouse area of what is now the city of Plymouth in Devon. Like Bertram Fletcher Robinson, who was also living in Devon at that same time, GTB is chiefly remembered for his association with ACD. However, GTB was a formidable character in his own right and had he lived beyond his early thirties, there seems little doubt that his name would have become more widely known.

Unfortunately, there has been a tendency to confuse GTB with other members of his family, in particular with two of his uncles, Dr George Budd and Dr John Wreford Budd. In the case of the first uncle, this confusion evidently stems from their shared name and profession. Confusion with the second uncle probably results from the fact that both men practised medicine in the Plymouth area within a decade of one another and each acquired a well-deserved reputation for an eccentric bedside manner. Furthermore, in 1858, a third uncle called Dr Samuel Budd of Exeter had a son and also named him George. This George Budd elected to study medicine during the early 1880s as had his grandfather, father, six uncles and at least two cousins before him, one of whom was GTB.

The association between GTB and ACD began whilst both men were studying medicine at Edinburgh University during 1879. Crucially, GTB was in his final year and some four years older than ACD. In 1882, GTB employed ACD as a junior partner at his surgery in the affluent town of East Stonehouse. During their brief medical partnership, ACD resided with GTB and his young wife in a splendid apartment overlooking Plymouth Hoe. However, ACD was concerned by his partner's unorthodox approach to medicine and soon departed, despite the fact that this placed him in both a precarious professional and financial position.

There is certainly something unusual about ACD's relationship with GTB. ACD was often forthright in his manner towards others and yet he was very circumspect in his treatment of GTB. For example on 22 February 1923, ACD revisited Plymouth and stayed at the Grand Hotel, just meters from where he had once lived with GTB. This trip clearly evoked memories because in November 1923, ACD had an article entitled *My First Experiences in Practice* published in *The Strand Magazine*. In October 1924, a slightly revised version of this article was republished as the sixth chapter in his autobiography. In both cases, ACD used the pseudonym 'Dr. James Cullingworth' to refer to GTB, despite the fact that his former friend and senior partner had died some thirty-five years before. It has been suggested that ACD adopted this approach in order to protect the reputation of GTB's descendents. This chapter aims to elaborate further upon what is already known about GTB and the nature of his relationship with ACD.

## 'Budding' Partners

GTB was born on 3 November 1855 at 28 Park Street, Clifton, Bristol (now *Blackwell's Bookshop* at 89 Park Street). He was one of nine children born to a successful and eminent physician, Dr William Budd, and his wife, Caroline (née Hilton). Both GTB and his elder brother Arthur James Budd (14 October 1853 – 27 August 1899) received their early education at Clifton College. On 4 October 1872, Arthur was admitted to Pembroke College at the University of Cambridge. Shortly thereafter, Dr William Budd developed a chronic cerebral disease from which he never fully recovered. In 1877, Arthur gained a Bachelor of Arts degree and then relocated to Edinburgh where GTB was already studying medicine.

Throughout his medical training (1875 – 1880), GTB played rugby for a Scottish team called Edinburgh Wanderers Rugby Football Club (see Plate 11). During the 1877/78 rugby season, Arthur Budd also represented 'Edinburgh Wanderers' and he became the team captain. In around March 1878, both brothers moved to London. GTB became a medical assistant and rented rooms from one Henry Henly at 11 Craven Street, The Strand, Westminster. Arthur enrolled himself as a medical student at the nearby St. Bartholomew's Hospital Medical College. Both brothers then played rugby for the famous Blackheath Football Club throughout the 1878/79 season (see Plate 12).

During 1879, GTB fell in love with a seventeen year old ward of chancery called Kate Russell (see Plate 13). She was a resident of an orphanage run by one Charles Chapman at 12 Percy Villas, Norwood, London. Kate had been born in 1862 at Windsor in Berkshire and her late father was an army officer called Major Gustavius Russell.

On 21 September 1879, GTB married the underage Kate at a registry office in The Strand, London. Their wedding ceremony was performed by the Superintendent Registrar, John Jeffrey and it was attended by two witnesses called Anthony Holt and Charles Greene. GTB falsely declared that he was a 'Civil Engineer' and Kate falsely declared that she was eighteen years-old.

Plate 11. Edinburgh Wanderers Rugby Football Club (1876/77). George Turnavine Budd is stood second from right.

The Blackheath Team, 1878-79.

A. Budd    F. S. Ireland    A. S. Maesuln    Aur. Spurling    G. Stones    H. C. Harkison    P. Brunskill    N. Smith
W. H. White    W. J. Penny    H. D. Batrson    L. Stokes    G. W. Burton    A. Poland    G. Budd
O. Richardson    G. Spurling    A. H. Jackson    R. Cuff    A. R. Layman

Plate 12.  Blackheath Football Club (1878/79).
The team featured both George Turnavine Budd
and his brother, Arthur James Budd.
THE PATRICK CASEY COLLECTION.

In October 1879, GTB returned to Edinburgh with his young wife and they befriended ACD.  Later, ACD wrote that the Budd's elopement had caused a 'scandal'.  He also reported that the newly-weds selected their honeymoon destination by searching *Bradshaw's Railway Companion* for a place that neither of them had visited before.  GTB reputedly tried to disguise himself by dyeing his hair black, but the dye took unevenly and produced a startling striped effect that did not wash out for years.  The newly-weds then rented 'four small rooms over a grocer's shop' in Edinburgh and ACD was compelled to sit on piles of medical books during visits to their sparsely furnished home.

29

Plate 13.  Kate Budd née Russell (1889).
COURTESY OF LESLEY & ROGER BACON.

During the 1879/80 rugby season, GTB emulated Arthur Budd by being appointed the captain of Edinburgh Wanderers. Over the course of that season, Edinburgh Wanderers played eight matches and lost five. It appears that ACD sometimes attended these games because he wrote that GTB was 'somewhat handicapped by the fury with which he played'. Meanwhile, Arthur had already played rugby for England on three occasions and he was to play a further two times. His final international was played on 19 March 1881 just thirteen months before GTB entered into medical partnership with ACD (see Plate 14). Later, ACD made the following comment about the rugby prowess of the Budd brothers in his autobiography although he does not refer to either of them directly by name:

> He [GTB] was up to international form, and his younger brother [sic] was reckoned by good judges to be about the best forward who ever donned the rose-embroidered jersey of England.

It is worth noting that ACD confused the respective ages of the Budd brothers within this description. This is perhaps understandable given that these lines were penned some forty-four years after he first met GTB. Arthur Budd served as a joint vice president of the Rugby Football Union between 1886 and 1888 and he was elected President for the 1888/1889 rugby season. On 30 September 1889, he chaired a meeting that led to the foundation of the London Society of Rugby Union Football Referees and he was elected its first ever secretary. In 1897, he also jointly authored a book entitled *Football* with Bertram Fletcher Robinson (see Chapter 4).

On 9 January 1880, Dr William Budd died aged sixty-eight years from complications relating to the cerebral disease that had first afflicted him during 1873. Shortly thereafter, his widow, Caroline May Budd, left the West Country to reside with Arthur Budd at 32 Charlesville Road, Fulham. Arthur was then employed as a solicitor indicating that he had withdrawn from his medical studies at St. Bartholomew's Hospital Medical College.

During August 1880, GTB was awarded both a first class Bachelors degree in Medicine and a Masters degree in Surgery from Edinburgh University. He then decided to relocate to Bristol in order to take over his father's once thriving practice. Unfortunately, William's chronic illness had necessitated frequent convalescent trips to France, Switzerland and the rural English counties. Perhaps for this reason, GTB found that the practice had sunk too low for it to be revived and before long he was deep in debt. Ironically, in 1965 a William Budd Health Centre was opened at Knowle West in Bristol and it is now one of the largest practices in that area.

In around March 1881, GTB sent a telegram to ACD imploring him to provide both help and advice. At that time, ACD was working as a medical assistant to Dr Reginald Hoare in Birmingham. Nevertheless, ACD travelled to Bristol and he advised GTB to meet with his creditors, explain his difficulties and offer to repay them after making a fresh start elsewhere. This GTB did, and either the creditors believed him, or his wealthy family rallied to his aid because by 3 April 1881, he was residing at East Stonehouse near Plymouth.

Plate 14. Arthur Budd in his 'rose-embroidered jersey'.
THE PATRICK CASEY COLLECTION.

32

## The Medical Partnership

In June 1881, GTB opened a surgery at his home at 1 Durnford Street in East Stonehouse. On 12 November of that same year, Kate gave birth to their first child, a daughter called Margaret. About that same time, GTB leased an adjacent coach house and stables at 10 Barrack Place. The site of GTB's former surgery was until recently marked with a commemorative plaque that was stolen during 2003 (see Plate 15).

This commemorative plaque erroneously overstated the duration of ACD's connection with GTB's surgery and the impact that this stay in Devon had upon his later work, *The Hound of the Baskervilles* (1901). However, in that story Sherlock Holmes does refer to a newspaper called the *Western Morning News*. ACD almost certainly read a regional newspaper entitled *The Western Morning News* during his seven-weeks as a junior medical partner to GTB at East Stonehouse in 1882.

Plate 15. The plaque that once marked
the site of 1 Durnford Street.
THE BRIAN PUGH COLLECTION.

The move to Durnford Street seemingly marked an upturn in GTB's fortunes because records reveal that on 16 November 1881 he also acquired a third lease for a property known as Higher Luxmore at Higher Leigham (near Eggbuckland on the outskirts of Plymouth). GTB agreed to pay an annual rent of £50 over a three-year period for this property that comprised of a large house, a stable, a coach house and more than three acres of meadowland. The tenancy was due to commence on Christmas Day 1881, but it is not known whether GTB ever actually resided at this address. In any event, during the spring of 1882, GTB sent ACD a telegram that read:

> Started here last June. Colossal success. Come down by next train if possible. Plenty of room for you. Splendid opening.

Clearly, GTB was desirous of an immediate response to this message because he quickly sent a second and more demanding telegram to ACD as follows:

> I have seen thirty thousand patients in the last year. My actual takings have been over four thousand pounds. All patients come to me. Would not cross the street to see Queen Victoria. You can have all the visiting, all surgery, all midwifery. Make what you like of it. Will guarantee three hundred pounds the first year.

ACD was reluctant to give up his job as a medical assistant in Birmingham. Nevertheless, he felt compelled to give GTB's proposition a try and so he duly travelled to Devon. Upon his arrival at Plymouth Railway Station, ACD was greeted by an exuberant GTB in an impressive horse-drawn carriage. This reception must have been remarkably different to the one that he had received upon his arrival in Bristol just some fourteen months before.

ACD was driven to the Budd residence at 6 Elliot Terrace on Plymouth Hoe. Clearly, between 16 November 1881 and early May 1882, GTB had leased this fourth property and relocated there with his family. ACD was duly impressed by this imposing six-storey Victorian mansion. However, upon closer inspection he discovered that the plush furnishings were confined to the first floor landing and that the rest of the house was unfurnished. GTB led ACD to believe that the entire property was his and that he would eventually refurbish it. Records now reveal that GTB merely co-leased this property with the nearby Royal Western Yacht Club and Grand Hotel. When ACD was shown to his bedroom he found it contained only a bed and a packing case, upon which stood a hand basin. GTB hammered some nails into the wall so that ACD might hang up his clothes.

ACD recalls in his autobiography that a strange incident occurred one evening after dinner. GTB encouraged him to hold up a small object and thereupon shot a dart at it with an airgun. GTB triumphantly exclaimed that he had hit plumb centre but ACD denied this and held up his finger with the dart sticking out of it as proof. GTB was so apologetic that ACD felt compelled to laugh-off the incident. Upon examining the small object further, ACD found it to be a medal that was inscribed thus: 'Presented to George Budd for Gallantry in Saving Life, January 1879'. ACD questioned GTB about this and was informed that his senior partner was presented with the medal for rescuing a drowning boy. ACD was prepared to be impressed but GTB dismissed the matter lightly. GTB told him that anyone could pull a child out of the water and that the tricky part had been getting him to enter it in the first place! GTB further added:

> Then there are the witnesses; four shillings a day I had to pay them, and a quart of beer in the evenings. You see you can't just pick up a child and carry it to the edge of a pier and throw it in. You'd have all sorts of complications from the parents.

Later, Kate Budd asked ACD not to take too much notice of her husband's bravado. She maintained that the medal had indeed been awarded to GTB for rescuing a boy from the ice, at great risk to his own life.

On another occasion, GTB suggested to ACD that they should publish a newspaper called *Scorpion* and then use it to 'sting' the Mayor and Corporation of Plymouth. GTB offered to write the political commentary and he proposed that ACD might contribute a serialised novel. The Mayor of Plymouth at that time was one John Shelley but it is unclear why GTB wished to publicly criticise him and other local officials.

ACD was also struck by the situation that greeted him at 1 Durnford Street and 10 Barrack Place. Both of these properties were filled to overflowing with waiting patients. Many of these people were probably former patients of GTB's uncle, Dr John Wreford Budd, who ran a popular practice at nearby 5 Princess Square until his death in 1873. The influence wielded by the Budd family in medical circles at this time cannot be underestimated. One young doctor, having failed several times to start a practice in Devon, lamented that one had to become a 'Buddist' in order to prosper in the county! Indeed, GTB's grandfather and several of his other uncles had also worked as physicians in Devon at Exeter and North Tawton (located seven miles north-east of Okehampton).

ACD observed that GTB lost no time in abusing his patients roundly. On one occasion, he reportedly refused to treat an obese patient on the grounds that he ate and drank too much. GTB advised this man to knock down a policeman, go to prison and return upon his release in the unlikely event that treatment was still required! On another occasion, he was consulted by a woman who complained of a 'sinking feeling'. GTB suggested that she might try drinking a glass of wine each day and then swallowing the cork because 'there's nothing better than cork when you are sinking.' ACD reflected that the scene was as good as any pantomime!

ACD was also struck by the sign on the surgery door that advertised free consultations. He asked GTB how he made any money and was told that whilst the consultations were free the medicines were not. Evidently, GTB was apt to over-prescribe drugs that were generally prepared and dispensed on-site by Kate Budd.

GTB provided ACD with a consultation room and promised him all home visits and surgery. However, after three weeks in practice, ACD had earned just 53 shillings (£2 12s. 12d.) and became doubtful as to whether he could make a living. GTB suggested that ACD was unduly timid and that people expected their doctor to bully them. However, this approach to patient care was not to ACD's taste.

## The Split and its Aftermath

GTB still had on-going obligations towards his creditors in Bristol. Furthermore, he had recently acquired a junior partner in the shape of ACD and also held four leases on properties in Durnford Street, Barrack Place, Higher Leigham and Elliot Terrace. The stress of these ever-spiralling financial commitments appears to have taken its toll on GTB's mental health because in a state of paranoia and self-denial, he accused ACD of ruining his business. ACD felt that this was grossly unfair and offered to leave, but GTB fell ill and so he remained to run the surgery. GTB appeared to be grateful and he offered to help ACD start his own practice elsewhere. However, unbeknown to ACD, the Budds had regularly intercepted letters that were sent to him by his mother, Mary Doyle. She perhaps intuitively, or advisedly, expressed the opinion that GTB was a bankrupt swindler and a blackguard. GTB did not read ACD's defensive replies and wrongly concluded that he shared his mother's sentiments. He then hatched an elaborate plot to turn the tables upon ACD. GTB's plan was to make ACD dependent upon a weekly gift of £1. Thereafter, GTB would discontinue his support in order that ACD might fail to meet any debts and be bankrupted. During June 1882, an unsuspecting ACD decided to start his own surgery and 'went prospecting to

Tavistock in Devon but could not see anything to suit'. He then decided to board a steamer for Portsmouth and appears to have arrived there sometime around 24 June.

By 1 July 1882, ACD had opened a surgery at 2 Bush Villas in Southsea in Hampshire. GTB wrote to ACD and accused him of writing hurtful comments to his mother. He claimed to have read scraps of torn-up letter found by Kate Budd in ACD's room. Coincidentally, ACD had the very same letter to which GTB referred in his pocket whilst he read his former partner's missive. GTB then discontinued all financial assistance to ACD. Ironically, though ACD did find it hard to make a good living as a doctor in both Southsea and, latterly, London, his financial difficulties were not prompted by the devious intents of GTB. Indeed it was fortunate that ACD did experience some hardship because he turned increasingly to writing in order to supplement his income.

Following the split, GTB's finances went from bad to worse. On 29 September 1882, he surrendered the lease on Higher Luxmore and was forced to pay £38 in compensation to his landlord, a farmer called Benjamin Butland of Leigham Barton, Eggbuckland. By 1885, GTB had also relinquished the lease for 6 Elliot Terrace and he was compelled to return with his growing family to 1 Durnford Street. This development must have been acutely embarrassing to a man who had previously made a point of walking through the professional district of Plymouth, clutching his day's takings in full view of other local physicians. GTB's reversal in fortunes undoubtedly stemmed from accumulating debts, exasperated by a dwindling practice. The reduction in patient numbers was probably caused by his practice of combining free consultations with the lavish over-prescription of drugs. GTB was reportedly criticised by the local coroner on more than one occasion for his lack of regard to the side effects of these drugs, although no case was ever brought against him.

GTB did not fare well with his personal affairs either. During the eight years that he and Kate lived together in the Plymouth area they had six children. These were, in order of their birth: Margaret (12 November 1881 – 1950), Diana (28 December 1882 – 1977), Iolanthe (January 1884 – 12 April 1967), Kate (28 November 1885 – 28 November 1885), Mildred (7 June 1887 – 3 February 1940) and William (30 April 1888 – 5 May 1888). Kate died just one hour after her birth from 'congestion of the lungs' and William (named after GTB's father) died aged five days because of 'debility from birth'. GTB certified both the birth and death of his only son. On 6 May 1888, William was buried at Ford Park Cemetery, Mutley, Plymouth. At about that same time, GTB became convinced that someone was trying to poison him. Consequently, he would often sit down to meals surrounded by complicated apparatus that was designed to test the food before he ate it.

In January 1889, just eight months after the death of William, GTB wrote his Last Will and Testament. This document was witnessed by a local solicitor, John G. Hellard and his clerk, John Howard. Both of these men were employed by the firm of Bewes, Hellard & Bewes in East Stonehouse. On 11 February 1889, Kate Budd paid £6 to Ford Park Cemetery in Plymouth for the freehold on the plot in which her son was buried. GTB died on 28 February 1889. The preceding events suggest that he was invalided and unable to work and that his death had been anticipated.

GTB's death was certified by one Dr C.A. Hingston. The official cause of death is recorded as 'Morbus Cerebri' (disease of the brain). It is notable that both GTB's father (William) and brother (Arthur) also died from brain diseases aged sixty-eight and forty-five years respectively. In 1995, a physician from Torquay called Dr David Nigel Pearce suggested that the underlying cause of GTB's dementia was either a brain tumour (meningioma) or more probably neurosyphilis (a sexually transmitted infection). The latter condition might also explain his striking appearance, violent mood swings and bouts of paranoia and depression.

GTB was buried within the same grave as his recently deceased son. Recent conservation work undertaken by cemetery staff in conjunction with the present authors has revealed that this grave contains a collapsed monumental surround. The edging of this surround comprises of sand, cement, slate and ceramic tiles that are similar to those used within the manufacture of Victorian fireplaces. The cemetery staff concluded that this monument was probably homemade, further supporting the view that GTB was suffering from a chronic ailment that precluded him from earning an income prior to his death.

GTB's death was announced in both *The Western Morning News* (2 March 1889), and *The Times* (4 March 1889). On 16 March, a short obituary was published in *The British Medical Journal*. It recalled that GTB had contributed the following three papers to that journal; *On Amyloid Degeneration*, *The Nature of Rheumatic Symptoms* and *Position of White Corpuscles*. The same article reports that GTB had made other contributions to *The Lancet* and that he was survived by a widow and four children.

GTB had stipulated that a friend called William Chilcott should act as one of two joint executors to his Last Will and Testament. William Chilcott was a 'Chief Fleet Engineer' at Her Majesty's Dockyard in Devonport. Perhaps he had assisted GTB in formulating many novel ideas for inventions that were all subsequently rejected by the local Admiralty Board? These plans included supplying body armour to prone soldiers and magnetic devices for deflecting cannon balls from naval ships. The other joint executor was GTB's uncle, Francis Nonus Budd, a Bristol-based barrister. However, Francis renounced this responsibility for reasons that perhaps related to his nephew's scandalous marriage.

GTB's estate was subsequently proved at £565.5s.0d gross and £186.18s.1d net. The large discrepancy between these two sums suggests that considerable payments were made to creditors and that GTB did indeed die in straitened circumstances. Kate Budd inherited the balance of GTB's estate.

After GTB's death, Kate Budd and her four surviving children, Margaret, Diana, Iolanthe and Mildred, remained at 1 Durnford Street with one Dr William E. Corbett. *The Plymouth, Devonport and Stonehouse Street Directory* indicates that Dr Corbett practised medicine at this address until about 1899. Corbett was twice elected Chairman of the East Stonehouse Urban District Council (1902-1904 and 1913-1914) and he oversaw the amalgamation of East Stonehouse with Plymouth on 1 November 1914. The same records reveal that Kate and her daughters left Durnford Street between 1892 and 1893. It is not known where they went initially. However, the 1901 English Census (31 March) lists a thirty-nine year old Berkshire born widow called Kate Budd as residing at 1 Douglas Road, Lewisham, London. She is recorded as 'living on her own means' with two Plymouth born daughters called Margaret and Mildred aged nineteen years and thirteen years respectively. Furthermore, the 1911 English Census (2 April) lists fifty year old Kate Budd and twenty-three year old Mildred as both 'living on their own means' at 17 Southbrook Road, Lee, Lewisham, London.

The fate of three of GTB's daughters has been determined. In 1906, Margaret Budd married one Roland Cunard Bentley, an 'assistant secretary to a public company'. The 1911 English Census lists the couple as living with their two children, Caroline Margaret and Hugh Roland Budd Bentley at 7 New Road, Bexleyheath, Kent. Shortly thereafter, the couple had a second son, John. During WWII, Iolanthe Budd met a New Zealander called Arthur Reynolds whilst she was serving as a nurse in France. In 1919, the couple married and relocated to New Zealand where they had two children, Iolanthe Joyce and Russell Arthur. On 23 September 1905, Diana Budd married Frederick Bacon and the couple then had three children: Diana Joyce (b. 13 September 1906), Winifred (b. 4 August 1909) and Frederick (b. 15 April 1915). Little is known about the fate of Mildred Budd but it appears that she died both unmarried and childless at the age of fifty-three years on 3 February 1940.

# A Challenging Legacy?

GTB appears to have made a profound impression upon ACD because he is featured in two of his books, thinly disguised as 'Dr. James Cullingworth'. The first of these is entitled *The Stark Munro Letters* and it was published by Longmans, Green and Co. Ltd. (1895). The second is ACD's autobiography, *Memories and Adventures*, which was published by Hodder & Stoughton (1924). In this later work, Cullingworth is described as follows:

> In person he was about 5ft 9in in height, perfectly built, with a bulldog jaw, bloodshot deep-set eyes, overhanging brows, and yellowish hair as stiff as wire, which spurted up above his brows. He was a man born for trouble and adventure...

During 1912, ACD's story *The Lost World* was published (see Plate 16). It features a larger than-life character called Professor George Edward Challenger. It is widely claimed that Professor Challenger was based upon Professor William Rutherford who taught both GTB and ACD at Edinburgh University. The novel's hero and narrator, Edward G. Malone, describes his first encounter with Challenger thus:

> His appearance made me gasp. I was prepared for something strange, but not for so overpowering a personality as this. It was his size, which took one's breath away - his size and his imposing presence. His head was enormous, the largest I have ever seen upon a human being. I am sure that his top-hat, had I ventured to don it, would have slipped over me entirely and rested on my shoulders. He had the face and beard, which I associate with an Assyrian bull; the former florid, the latter so black as almost to have a suspicion of blue, spade-shaped and rippling down over his chest. The hair was peculiar, plastered down in front in a long, curving wisp over his massive

forehead. The eyes were blue-grey under great black tufts, very clear, very critical, and very masterful. A huge spread of shoulders and a chest like a barrel were the other parts of him which appeared above the table, save for two enormous hands covered with long black hair.

Despite the obvious physical differences between Challenger and 'Dr Cullingworth' both characters do share some striking personality traits. For example, Challenger has 'a bellowing, roaring, rumbling voice' and is forthright when interviewed. Similarly, Cullingworth is inclined to bully his patients during consultations by shouting abuse at them. Both Cullingworth and Challenger might also be viewed as scientific egotists who are apt to devise ingenious contraptions. Furthermore, both are disliked by their peers and marginalised within their respective professions. Hence it is possible that ACD partly based the character of Challenger upon GTB as well as Rutherford.

ACD published three novels that feature Professor Challenger: *The Lost World* (1912), *The Poison Belt* (1913) and *The Land of Mist* (1925). All three of these stories were originally serialised in *The Strand Magazine* (April – November 1912, March – July 1913 and July 1925 – March 1926 respectively). These tales were followed-up by two related short stories entitled *When the World Screamed* and *The Disintegration Machine* that also made their first appearance in *The Strand Magazine* (April/May 1928 and January 1929 respectively). These last two tales were republished in *The Maracot Deep and Other Stories* (1929).

There have been seven theatrical films featuring the character of Professor George Edward Challenger and at least one television series. The first film was *The Lost World* (1925) and it starred Wallace Beery as Challenger. The most recent film entitled *King of the Lost World* was made during 2005 and it starred Bruce Boxleitner as Challenger. Hence, the fictional character of Professor Challenger seems set to retain his place in popular culture. Perhaps he seems all the more real because ACD based him partly on GTB?

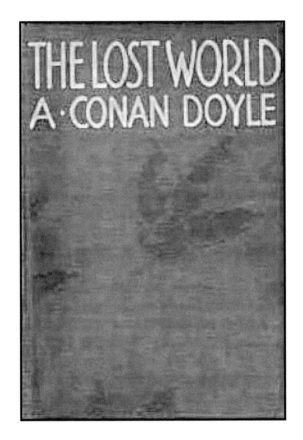

Plate 16. The cover for the very rare first issue
paperback edition of *The Lost World* by Sir
Arthur Conan Doyle (London, New York,
Toronto: Hodder and Stoughton, 1912).

# CHAPTER THREE

## Sir George Newnes
### (13 March 1851 – 9 June 1910)

Plate 17.  Sir George Newnes (circa 1905).
COURTESY OF JOHN TRAVIS ©1997.

# Introduction

George Newnes (hereafter GN) is best known as a pioneer of the New Journalism: the publishing of mass-circulation newspapers intended to entertain as well as inform (see Plate 17). More specifically, he is remembered also as the man who turned ACD and Sherlock Holmes into internationally-known figures. GN was born in Matlock on 13 March 1851, the youngest of the six children of Thomas Mold Newnes, a Congregational minister, and Sarah Newnes (née Urquhart). The father was a deeply religious and scholarly man, but with a sense of fun. By contrast, Mrs Newnes appears to have been an unconventional independent-minded lady, but one able to impose discipline when called for. It was hoped that GN would follow in his father's footsteps, and so when only nine years old he entered Silcoates School, a Yorkshire boarding school for the sons of Congregational ministers. Later, he attended Shireland Hall in Birmingham, and spent two terms at the City of London School, where against competition including the future British Prime Minister, Herbert Asquith, GN won a prize for story writing. Abandoning all hope of his son ever becoming a minister, his father arranged for a five-year apprenticeship to a London haberdasher. The young GN was well thought of, and was admired particularly for his skill with figures. When not at work he would browse the London bookshops and newsagents. While doing so he may have realised how little suitable reading material there was for the newly-literate working class that was created by the 1870 Education Act.

# The 'Newnes' Journalism

In around 1872, GN moved to Manchester where he managed a haberdashery shop for a different company. It is said that it was there that he was inspired to embark upon a career within publishing. He was struck by a report in a local newspaper: turning to his wife, Priscilla (née Hillyard), whom he married in 1875, he said 'That is what I call a real tit-bit. Now why cannot a paper be brought out containing nothing but tit- bits like this?'

There is some doubt as to when this germinal episode in GN's life occurred and also over the content of the article. In a biography, published shortly after GN's death and based on not only personal knowledge but also notes written by GN for an intended autobiography, no date is given but it is stated that the report that so aroused GN was of two station master's children who climbed aboard a railway carriage. The attached engine then started off, despite no driver being on board. Fortunately, it was possible to stop the runaway train and the children escaped unscathed. The entry concerning GN in the *Dictionary of National Biography* states that he read the article in the *Manchester Evening News* of 24 August 1881 and that it concerned a runaway train. Such a report did indeed appear, and the incident was noted also in the *Manchester Times* of three days later. GN, however, told a reporter from *The Idler* magazine in 1893 that the article was published in 1880, but apparently did not elaborate. Whenever and whatever its stimulus, the idea took hold; but GN was unable to find financial backing. Realising that he needed to raise the money himself, he opened a vegetarian café in a Manchester cellar. The early biographer quotes from a letter written by GN concerning its success. This is dated 13 March 1881, adding support to GN's recollection that the newspaper report that so aroused him appeared in 1880. On the other hand, it throws confusion over what the Manchester newspaper article was about. A plausible resolution is that the article of August 1881, and the remark to his wife, inspired the name of a magazine that GN had already in mind since whatever it was that he read a year earlier.

When the first issue of *Tit-Bits* materialised in October 1881, some 5,000 copies were sold in the first two hours (see Plate 18). Nevertheless, all was not plain sailing. Many, particularly those familiar with British sexual slang, were suspicious of the new weekly newspaper. Thanks to imaginative advertising, pockets of resistance were overcome and *Tit-Bits* became a national newspaper. After three years, GN moved its headquarters to London. Innovative readers' offers and competitions helped to swell the weekly circulation of *Tit-Bits* to 850,000 and it contributed £50,000 to GN's annual income. Encouraged by the success of *Tit-Bits*, GN embarked upon other publishing ventures. Not all, however, were a success. He disposed of his interest in the *Review of Reviews* to his collaborator William Thomas Stead (see Plate 19), a fellow-pupil at Silcoates and now a leading journalist, after only six months as the two seldom saw eye to eye. The Liberal-supporting *Westminster Gazette* ran at a loss and was eventually sold. The *Daily Courier* and a Sunday newspaper, the *Weekly Dispatch*, both failed to usurp their rivals. On the other hand, this was more than compensated for by the success of *Country Life*, *Woman's Life,* the *World-Wide Magazine* and, above all others, *The Strand Magazine*.

In addition to his provocative approach to journalism, W. T. Stead is also remembered as a staunch Spiritualist. It was in this respect that he became well acquainted with ACD and is said to have acted as both his 'collaborator and combatant' in relation to Spiritualist matters. Stead also appears to have known Bertram Fletcher Robinson (see Chapter 4). For example, he is favourably portrayed as a character called the 'Good Fairy' in a satirical playlet that was jointly written by Fletcher Robinson and P.G. Wodehouse and published in *Vanity Fair* (1904). Moreover, Stead was reported to have related a tale about a malevolent Egyptian coffin-lid to a small group of fellow first-class passengers in the smoking room of the *R.M.S. Titanic* shortly before it sank and he was lost (15 April 1912). This tale resembles a story about the 'Unlucky Mummy' exhibit at the British Museum that Fletcher Robinson had conceived whilst working as a journalist for the *Daily Express* newspaper during

1904. This story was never published hence, if it were the basis for Stead's tale aboard *Titanic*, Fletcher Robinson may have imparted it to him directly.

Plate 18. The cover of *Tit-Bits* (28 February 1891).

Plate 19. W. T. Stead (circa 1910).

# 'Newnes' Enterprises

When GN sold his interest in *Review of Reviews* he was anxious that the extra staff he took on should not suffer and so sought other ventures to keep them in work. Influenced by Herbert Greenhough Smith, who was to become its editor (see page 80), GN decided to publish a monthly magazine devoted to well-illustrated short stories. The response to *The Strand Magazine* exceeded even that following the launch of *Tit-Bits*. When it first appeared in January 1891, the entire print run of 300,000 sold out. Within a short time, its monthly circulation increased to half a million copies and thousands of short stories were being submitted for consideration.

In around June 1891, ACD also submitted two stories to *The Strand Magazine* that each featured Sherlock Holmes, *A Scandal in Bohemia* and *The Red-Headed League*. Greenough Smith was immediately impressed and thrust them before GN. Sharing his editor's enthusiasm, GN purchased without delay the rights to these stories and to several other ACD works that had already been published. During the 1920s, Greenhough Smith gave the following account of the circumstances that surrounded these events:

> I at once realised that here was the greatest short story writer since Edgar Allen Poe. I remember rushing into Mr Newnes's [sic] room and thrusting the stories before his eyes...Here, to an editor jaded with wading through reams of impossible stuff, comes a gift from Heaven, a godsend in the shape of the story that brought a gleam of happiness into the despairing life of this weary editor. Here was a new and gifted story-teller: there was no mistaking the ingenuity of the plot, the limpid clearness of the style, the perfect art of telling a story.

Although ACD owed much to *The Strand Magazine*, the converse also applied. During the eight-part serialisation of *The Hound of the Baskervilles* an extra 30,000 copies were sold each month.   The final development, of around 1897, was GN embarking upon the publication of popular books, a number intended to improve the knowledge and skills of the working classes.   The company founded by GN went on to publish many well-loved works by such as Richmal Crompton, Enid Blyton and P.G. Wodehouse (Bertram Fletcher Robinson's friend).

GN had activities outside of publishing too.   Some were undertaken with profit in mind; others were philanthropic.   For example, GN took a keen interest in scientific developments, and gave financial backing, to the tune of £38,000, to the pioneering Norwegian Antarctic explorer Carsten Egeberg Borchgrevink's expedition of 1898 to 1900.   This was against indifference, if not opposition, from the British geographical establishment.   Despite GN and Borchgrevink emphasising the British nature of the expedition, it would be some time before their efforts were acknowledged.   In the meantime, GN could rest content knowing that he now had an eponymous promontory, Newnes Land, and that Lady Newnes' Bay was named after his wife.   Yet more pleasurable was Borchgrevink's gift of the sledge-dog *Erebus*.   He proved one of GN's most devoted pets and certainly more entertaining than additional gifts that included a stuffed penguin!

Antarctica is not the only region housing places named after GN.   What is now a ghost town in Australia's New South Wales also bears his surname.   In 1905, GN, realising that many were coming to share his liking for the motor car and hearing of deposits of fuel-bearing shale in the Capertee Valley of New South Wales, set up the Commonwealth Oil Corporation to purchase the nearby shale mine in the Wolgan Valley.   The settlement that grew by the mine was named Newnes.   The venture was not a success and it cost GN some £240,000. Attempts were made to resume production after repeated industrial action led to the mine's closure in 1912, but all failed. Apart from a hotel patronised by tourists and trekkers, little exists of the settlement that served the mineworkers and their families.   On the other hand, some of the retorts at the mine can still be seen and the tunnel through which the Newnes railway link once ran is visited frequently for its fauna and is now known as the Glowworm Tunnel.

GN's other commercial enterprises included a brief involvement in early cinema and a heavy financial interest in the French car manufacturers, Darracq. As noted below, he also invested in ventures concerning his Devon home in Lynton. Gifts included an electric tramway in his birthplace, Matlock, and a public library to serve the less well-off of those living near his London mansion, Wildcroft in Putney Heath. In Lynton, GN paid for a Town Hall and a Congregational (now United Reformed) Church. Again, these are mentioned below.

GN also took part in national politics. During 1885, he was elected as the Liberal Member of Parliament for Newmarket, but lost the seat in the election of 1895. In 1900, he re-entered Parliament as the representative of the safe Liberal seat of Swansea, retiring due to ill-health in 1910. Despite his energetic personality and concern for the well-being of his fellowmen, GN made little impact in the House of Commons, his main claim to fame being that he was one of the best-dressed MPs. When he was awarded his baronetcy in 1895, it was not for his legislative efforts but as a press magnate who lent willing support to the Liberal Party cause.

GN's life was not always a happy one. During 1889, his ten year old son 'Artie' died and the resulting anguish is said to have turned his hair prematurely grey. More distressing, at least for his family, friends and colleagues, was GN's last years being bedevilled by diabetes and alcoholism. The last probably led to his frequent unexplained absences from home for days on end. It was largely due to his public drunkenness that plans to grant GN a peerage were dropped. GN died on 9 June 1910 at Lynton and is buried there. Whether due to life-long generosity, the effect of illness on his judgement, or both, he left many debts unpaid. His estate of some £175,000 by no means covered these. Lady Newnes never received her bequeathed annuity, and Frank Newnes spent most of his life paying off his father's debts.

# 'The English Riviera'

Although GN is still commemorated as an inhabitant of Lynton, this was not his first Devon home. During the late 1880s and the 1890s he had a winter residence in a fashionable part of the resort town of Torquay: Hesketh House, 15 Hesketh Crescent (see Plate 20) and now part of the Osborne Hotel, lies at the eastern end of an attractive crescent commissioned by the Palk family and built in 1848-9 to the design of the architects William and John Harvey. Named originally after Meadfoot Beach which it overlooks, it was soon redesignated as Hesketh Crescent to commemorate the birth of the first son to Maria Palk, née Hesketh. The Palks were leading landowners and responsible for much of the Victorian development of Torquay and her harbour. Unfortunately, due to lack of business acumen and a general profligacy, the Palk fortunes declined. In 1887, Hesketh Crescent was put up for auction but failed to make the reserve. It has proved difficult to ascertain when GN acquired Hesketh House, but he may well have stepped in when the property was left unsold at auction. *Kelly's* county directory of 1889 lists him as the occupier, as do those of 1893 and 1897. It is similarly difficult to gauge how much time GN spent in Torquay. A local weekly publication, *The Torquay Directory and South Devon Journal*, included lists of those visiting Torquay, but makes scant mention of the Newnes family. It is known that GN valued peace and privacy. A London press magnate would have no difficulty in persuading a small provincial publisher to keep his name out of the press.

Until it declined in popularity towards the close of the Nineteenth Century, Torquay was patronised by Victorian royalty, aristocracy and leading figures in the worlds of politics, art and science. The last included Charles Darwin who stayed at Hesketh Crescent in the summer of 1861. It seems unlikely that GN joined what at times was a glittering social scene. On his own admission he was a far better host than guest and would often go out of his way to avoid social invitations. Instead, he preferred to spend time in yachting, motoring, walking or enjoying a game of tennis or round of golf. On the other hand, it was far from a matter of all play and no work. It was while staying at Hesketh House that GN received and dealt with a letter from W.T. Stead containing his proposal for what was to become the *Review of Reviews*.

Plate 20. Hesketh House (*The Idler*: March 1893).

## 'England's Little Switzerland'

What in Victorian times came to be known as *England's Little Switzerland* consists of two adjacent villages: Lynton sitting at the top of a cliff and Lynmouth nestling below by the sea. Until the closing years of the Eighteenth Century, Lynmouth was a small, but successful, fishing and trading post. Fortunately for the residents, a precipitate fall in local fishing stock coincided with the Napoleonic Wars. Gentry and aristocracy accustomed to the European Grand Tour now had to seek pleasure and enlightenment much closer to home. Lynmouth soon became known as an attractive place to visit and stay at, and the village grew in size and prosperity. Building land, however, was at a premium and it became necessary to erect hotels and other tourist facilities in Lynton, which expanded during Victorian and Edwardian times from an insignificant farming village into a major, albeit somewhat select, tourist venue.

GN paid his first visit to Lynton in September 1887 at the invitation of an old friend and fellow chess enthusiast, Thomas Hewitt. Hewitt, later Sir Thomas, was a successful London lawyer who spent his summers at Lynton in a house built for him on North Walk. GN and his wife developed a fondness for Lynton and Lynmouth and during the next three years spent holidays there in rented houses. They soon decided on a permanent residence, and in 1890 GN purchased Hollerday Hill with the intention of building a mansion on the site. The work was to be supervised by a local builder called Bob Jones. Construction of the approach road, deliberately turning and twisting so as to spare the horses too steep an incline, began in May 1891. The building of Hollerday House commenced some eighteen months later (see Plate 21) and was completed by the end of 1893 at an estimated cost of £10,000 (see Plate 22). From then on, the Newnes spent each August, September and Christmas at their Lynton retreat. This was to the delight of many local people who, because of the debacle over the proposed pier (see below), feared that they were being abandoned by their benefactor. When GN became seriously ill in the summer of 1909, it was decided that he would leave Putney Heath to recuperate at Hollerday House. Nonetheless, his health deteriorated and GN died there less than a year later.

Plate 21. The Workmen that built Hollerday House.
COURTESY OF JOHN TRAVIS ©1997.

55

Plate 22. Hollerday House in Lynton (circa 1907).
COURTESY OF JOHN TRAVIS ©1997.

Because GN left substantial debts his son and widow decided to leave Hollerday House. The furniture was sold off at auction, but the house and surrounding land failed to attract any buyers. Hollerday House was shut down and left to its fate. On the night of 4 August 1913 the building caught fire and could not be saved. Although there was ample evidence of arson, the culprit has never been identified. Many blamed the Suffragettes, but nothing has been found to substantiate that claim. In April 1933, the Hollerday estate was purchased by John Holman and gifted to the people of Lynton and Lynmouth. The ruins of the house became a favourite place among the local children, but were put to more serious use during WWII as a Civil Defence training area. After the war the building was in a dangerous condition and considered to be in need of demolition. In the early 1950s, Hollerday House was blown up as part of a commando training exercise.

# A 'Newnes' Transport Policy

People and goods could reach Lynmouth by sea and Lynton by land, but for centuries transfer between the two was an arduous matter for both man and beast. Hewitt had an interest in rectifying this, and procured an Act of Parliament for building an esplanade and pier in Lynmouth and a cliff railway linking it with Lynton. It may well be that his invitation to GN was not based entirely on friendship. On the other hand, it is perhaps too unkind to suggest that Hewitt took advantage of his guest's concern for equine welfare. Whatever Hewitt's motives, GN took an almost instant interest in the suggested cliff railway and he agreed to provide the bulk of the funding. Bob Jones was commissioned to undertake the building work to a design that was drawn-up by the noted engineer, George Croydon Marks (later Baron Marks of Woolwich). By December 1887, the work was well under way. During February 1890, when almost completed, the railway carried its first cargo to the top of the cliff: a shipment of cement brought into Lynmouth (see Plate 23).

The Lynton and Lynmouth Cliff Railway was formally declared open by Mrs Jeune (the Lady of the Manor) on 7 April 1890 (Easter Monday). The railway consists of 860ft of dual track with a gauge of 45in and a gradient of 1:1.76. The two carriages are linked by a chain which passes around a wheel at the top of the railway and they operate on a counter-balance system, using water held in seven-hundred gallon tanks underneath them as the weight. When a carriage reaches the bottom of the cliff water is drawn off until it becomes lighter than that at the top. The upper carriage then embarks on a controlled descent, pulling the lower carriage up to the top of the railway where the tank can be refilled. For well over a century the 'Cliff Railway' has had an exemplary safety record and it has provided an invaluable service, both as a local amenity and as a much-patronised tourist attraction.

Plate 23. Lynton and Lynmouth Cliff Railway (1890).
From left to right: George Newnes, Bob
Jones and C. Andrews (driver).
THE SADRU BHANJI COLLECTION.

The Cliff Railway was not the only local transport venture involving GN. Once established as tourist resorts, Lynton and Lynmouth were well-served by horse-drawn passenger coaches. Nevertheless, they suffered from being remote from the railway and in the 1850s the local residents began to ask that Lynton and Lynmouth be served by a railway link. Due to commercial and bureaucratic obstacles nothing was achieved until 1894 when GN, Thomas Hewitt, A.B. Jeune and W.H. Halliday organised a series of meetings at which it was proposed that a narrow gauge

(1ft 11½in) railway be built between Barnstaple and Lynton. Despite an opposing proposal involving a standard gauge line, GN and his colleagues won over both local and Parliamentary opinion, and the Lynton and Barnstaple Railway Act was granted Royal Assent on 27 June 1895. GN became chairman of the board and in September 1895, Lady Newnes cut the first sod at what was to be Lynton Station. Unfortunately, the optimism epitomised by that evening's firework display at Hollerday House was not to be justified. Some landowners refused to sell their land or demanded a high price. There were arguments also over who would build the stations, as well as delays in laying the track. It was not until May 1898 that the line was finally opened (see Plate 24).

The new railway link ran from Barnstaple Town Station, which replaced the London and South Western Railway's Barnstaple Quay Station, to Lynton Station, with stops at Snapper Halt, Chelfham, Bratton Fleming, Blackmoor Gate, Parracombe Halt, Woody Bay and Caffyns Halt. The distance covered amounted to nearly twenty miles. The opening of the railway was not the end of the Company's problems. Costs had already increased well beyond the original estimate and one of the contractors was demanding payment of some £40,000. The latter involved the Company in legal action which was settled in its favour only on appeal. The precarious financial state was not helped by the public's attitude to the railway. Although some complained that the carriages were unsteady, most were concerned about the time taken to complete the journey (around ninety minutes instead of the predicted one hour) and also the remoteness of Lynton Station from the centre of the village. Trains did not run as frequently as originally proposed and the timetable was often inconvenient for connections with mainline trains at Barnstaple. The building of a viaduct across the Lyn Valley could have improved matters, but was turned down by GN, largely upon aesthetic grounds.

During 1903, in an attempt to improve the demand for and access to the railway, GN established a motor coach service between Ilfracombe and Blackmoor Gate. He was soon to withdraw this facility when one of his drivers exceeded the speed limit of 8mph and was fined, a step which angered GN. Increasing competition from motor transport and escalating running costs served only to worsen the railway's financial plight and, in 1923, the board sold out to the Southern Railway. The new owners refurbished the stations, track and rolling stock and brought about improvements to the timetable. Nevertheless, the line continued to lose money and was closed down in 1935, the last train leaving Lynton at 7.55pm on 30 September. The track was removed swiftly and rolling stock scrapped or sold off. Some of the stations were allowed to fall derelict; others are now private houses. The station at Lynton can still be seen and although now a domestic building retains some of the platform at the rear. As to the future, the Lynton and Barnstaple Railway Association was formed in 1979 with the intention of eventually reopening as much of the line as possible. A restored Woody Bay Station now sits at the head of a mile or so of track, along which excursions are run during the summer.

Plate 24. The Lynton and Barnstaple
Railway in operation (circa 1900).
THE SADRU BHANJI COLLECTION.

Were it not for GN, Lynton and Lynmouth could well have had a second railway station. On the day that the Lynton and Barnstaple Railway opened, GN declared his opposition to a proposed Cardiff-backed railway between Minehead and Lynmouth. Holiday-makers and day-trippers from Wales would travel to Minehead by steamer and thence to Lynmouth by railway. Realising that the railway could be in competition with the Lynton and Barnstaple Railway and also determined to retain the resort's exclusive character, GN threatened never to visit Lynton and Lynmouth again if the Minehead railway line was built.

## Something Old, Something 'Newnes'

When his son, Frank, came of age in 1897, GN not only held a magnificent party and firework display at Hollerday House, but also ensured a more lasting commemoration. One of the obstacles to the smooth running of local affairs had long been the lack of any permanent place where councillors could meet. During October 1897, their deliberations in a rented room at Gordon Villas were interrupted by Bob Jones bearing news of a telegram from GN stating that he had purchased a plot of land and intended building a town hall there. The offer was grasped and the foundation stone laid on 11 May 1898 by Lady Newnes who earlier that day had declared the Lynton and Barnstaple Railway open. The building of Lynton Town Hall took two years to complete, at a personal cost to GN of some £20,000. Fittingly, it was GN who performed the opening ceremony on 15 August 1900. Although displaying a mixture of architectural styles, the building is not unattractive; and, despite concern from time to time over its state, continues to serve the community and visitor well (see page 206). In addition to being available for various public functions it houses a permanent exhibition devoted to GN. It also houses two busts of GN: one recently placed in an outside niche, the other given pride of place on the main staircase (see Plate 25). The latter was a gift from the local people and it was unveiled at a ceremony that was attended by ACD in September 1902 (see Plate 26). He was a guest at Hollerday House at the time, and judging from a letter written from there was feeling better for a pleasant few days and looking forward to hunting with the Devon Stag Hounds in the nearby Doone Valley.

Plate 25. The bust of Sir George Newnes inside Lynton Town Hall.
THE BRIAN PUGH COLLECTION.

TRIBUTE TO SIR G. NEWNES.—In recognition of his services to the village, and particularly of the building of the Town-hall, the inhabitants of Lynton subscribed for a bust of Sir George Newnes, which was unveiled on Saturday. There was a large gathering at the ceremony, which was performed by Mrs. Hewitt, wife of Mr. J. Hewitt, K.C. Sir A. Conan Doyle, in the course of a speech on the occasion, referred to the influence which Sir George Newnes had had upon the literature of the country. It had not been sufficiently recognized how some 15 or 20 years ago, when the new Education Act had just prepared a number of readers who were all anxious to get something to read, and who were not sufficiently educated to study the very deepest and very thickest volumes, Sir George, with extraordinary sagacity and foresight, came forward and provided for them just that class of literature which at the same time interested them, elevated them, and did them good. They had only at the present day to compare any bookstall on the boulevards of Paris with any in England, the wholesome food they got in this country with the absolute garbage supplied in Paris, to see what a man like Sir George and his imitators had done for the public of this country, a most important thing striking deeply into the very roots of national life.

Plate 26. A report from *The Times* newspaper about the speech that was given by Arthur Conan Doyle to mark the unveiling of the Newnes bust (9 September 1902).

By the beginning of the Twentieth Century, the Lynton Congregational Church built in 1850 had become too small and was inconveniently sited for many of the worshippers. In 1903, Bob Jones offered a plot of land on which a new church could be built in Lee Road. Realising that their own efforts would be unlikely to raise the required funding, the congregation approached GN for help. With characteristic generosity and in memory of his father, he embarked on paying some £1,500, not only for the site to be enlarged but also for a far more imposing building than planned. The new Congregational (now United Reformed) Church opened for worship in August 1904. The opening services were taken by the well-known London preacher, the Revd Reginald John Campbell (see Plate 27). With typical liberality, GN presented him with a new motor car.

Plate 27. Sir George Newnes (right) and the
Revd R. J. Campbell leaving the Lynton
Congregational Church (1904).
COURTESY OF JOHN TRAVIS ©1995.

The above were not the only local amenities sponsored by GN.
He also subsidised the hydroelectric plant on the East Lyn River
that came into operation in 1890, and the new waterworks,
which he declared open in 1904. As to leisure activities, during
1891, GN, a keen cricket lover, paid for Warren field in the
Valley of Rocks to be levelled and converted into a cricket
pitch. Three years later, he opened a new golf course at
Martinhoe Common that he had helped pay for. In 1905, GN
purchased Summit Castle. It was demolished under the
watchful eye of Tom Jones (brother of Bob Jones) and the site
turned into a bowling green.

# A Man of Contradictions

GN was a man of contrasting facets. The son and grandson of Congregational ministers, and educated as such, he nevertheless turned to commerce as a career. Although best remembered for his accomplishments, by no means did all GN touch turn to gold. Even within his prime field of expertise, publishing, many of his ventures cannot be counted as successes. GN turned ACD into an internationally renowned author, but in the years up to his death the profits of his flagship company, 'George Newnes Ltd.', were plummeting. His decision to invest in the car manufacturers, Darracq, was a wise one; but not that to reinvest in a Peruvian rubber concern. Another overseas venture, the Commonwealth Oil Corporation also cost GN dearly.

GN was also capable of dramatic U-turns within his thinking. For example, during his speech at the opening of the Lynton and Lynmouth Cliff Railway, GN announced his offer to build a pier. This undertaking was welcomed and it resulted in much local property speculation and building activity in preparation for an influx of tourists who could now arrive by steamer. This burst of endeavour was further fuelled by GN's purchase of Hollerday Hill. There was much shock, if not outrage, when in February 1892, GN let it be known that he was no longer interested in building a pier. The reasons for this change of heart are obscure. It may have been due to a dispute over the purchase of the necessary land. Alternatively, it has been suggested that GN had come to value the peace and privacy that *Little Switzerland* offered and had no wish for this to be spoiled by hordes of tourists. Later, when the Lynton and Barnstaple Railway came into being, GN was among those hoping that any desire for a pier would now vanish. He was to be bitterly disappointed. Pressure for a pier continued and the local council voted to give way. The esplanade was extended appropriately, but this was as far as the development went. Ironically, the proposal to build a pier was finally dropped in 1900, much to the relief of GN – the original proponent of the scheme!

Although his family's arrival was usually marked with much celebration and GN is still commemorated as a benefactor of Lynton and Lynmouth, not all welcomed his presence there. The Lynton and Lynmouth Cliff Railway was and still is a success, and both the Lynton Town Hall and Lynton United Reformed Church remain valued community assets. By contrast, the Lynton and Barnstaple Railway failed to live up to its promise. GN's decision to withdraw his support for a pier caused much anger, particularly among the business community. Some would have been further outraged by his opposition to a second railway link with Minehead. In his general dealings, sometimes a hard-headed business-like attitude would prevail; by contrast, at other times he would display almost reckless generosity. The extravagant funding of an Antarctic expedition and the gift of a motorcar to the Revd R. J. Campbell are noted above. Another example was the unconditional gift of some £600 worth of shares in George Newnes Ltd. to ACD in 1897. Although by no means averse to public show of wealth, and a gifted after-dinner speaker, GN would nonetheless avoid social events. A flair for publicity was what served GN best; but had to be reconciled with a desire for quiet privacy. Perhaps the saddest contradiction is that a man so concerned about the moral welfare of those less fortunate, should die with a growing reputation as a man no longer able to control his drinking.

# CHAPTER FOUR

## Bertram Fletcher Robinson
### (22 August 1870 – 21 January 1907)

Plate 28.    Bertram Fletcher Robinson (circa 1906).

# Introduction

Bertram Fletcher Robinson (hereafter BFR) was born on the 22 August 1870 at 80 Rose Lane, Mossley Vale, Wavertree, West Derby, Lancashire (see Plate 28). He was the only child of forty-three year old Joseph Fletcher Robinson (1827-1903) and his second wife, twenty-nine year old Emily Robinson née Hobson (1841-1906). Joseph was a successful self-made man and three years before Bertram's birth he had founded a merchant business in Liverpool that still prospers there today. BFR's paternal grandfather, Richard Robinson, was born on 10 July 1797 at Hallford in Lancashire and he received his education at the nearby Blackburn Academy. In around 1823, Richard was ordained as an independent minister and was given a ministry at Witham in Essex. Joseph Fletcher Robinson was named after the Revd Joseph Fletcher who had taught Richard Robinson at Blackburn Academy. Joseph's brother was Sir Richard John Robinson (1828-1903), the long-time editor of the London *Daily News* newspaper and a prominent member of the committee of the Reform Club, Pall Mall, London.

## Aside from the 'Baskerville Legend'

BFR received his early schooling at a small boarding school called Penkett Road Beach House at Liscard in West Cheshire. In around 1882, Joseph Fletcher Robinson retired and relocated with his family to Ipplepen in Devon. Between April 1882 and April 1890, BFR was enrolled as a day boy at nearby Newton College Proprietary School in Newton Abbot. This school specialised in preparing boys for a career in either the British Army or Anglican Church and it enjoyed an excellent reputation for competitive sports. During his time as a pupil at 'Newton College', BFR was awarded prizes for his achievements in 'Divinity', 'English', 'History' and 'Sport'. He was also elected '2nd Captain School-House' (a senior Prefect) and editor of the school journal, *The Newtonian* (1887-1889).

In April 1890, BFR was admitted to Jesus College at the University of Cambridge. Over the next four years, he played as a forward in three annual Oxbridge 'Varsity Rugby Matches (1892-1894) and reportedly would have played for England but for an "accident". During 1893, BFR was appointed sub-editor of an undergraduate magazine called *The Granta* and was also awarded a History degree. The following year, BFR made the Cambridge 'Trial VIII' ahead of the annual Oxbridge 'Varsity Boat Race and he passed Part I of the Law Tripos degree. On 17 June 1896, BFR accepted an invitation to the Bar at the Inner Temple thereby qualifying as a barrister-at-law. During 1897, he began writing for *Cassell's Family Magazine* and was also awarded a Master of Arts degree by his Alma Mater.

Between 1892 and 1907, BFR wrote or edited at least three hundred items for various books, journals and newspapers. These writings included four playlets that were jointly written with his friend, P.G. Wodehouse (1881-1975), and a series of eight short stories that were republished in a book, *The Chronicles of Addington Peace* (London: Harper & Brother, June 1905). This book is listed in the influential *Queen's Quorum: A History of the Detective-Crime Short Story as Revealed by the 106 Most Important Books Published in this Field Since 1845* (Boston: Little, Brown & Co., 1951). Between May 1904 and October 1906, BFR edited some one-hundred and twenty-six issues of the popular weekly periodical, *Vanity Fair*. Shortly before he died in 1907, BFR was appointed editor of an illustrated weekly periodical entitled *The World – A Journal for Men and Women*. It was managed by ACD's friend, Max Pemberton, and owned by Lord Northcliffe, a former employee of GN (see Chapter 3).

## 'Cementing' the Foundations

During 1900, the British public developed an insatiable appetite for news concerning The Second Boer War in South Africa (1899-1902). This climate prompted another former GN employee, Cyril Arthur Pearson, to introduce a new daily newspaper. The first edition of Pearson's *Daily Express* was published on 24 April 1900 and it became the first British daily newspaper to put news on its front page. BFR was employed by Pearson to work as one of his 'Seven War Correspondents in South Africa'. In March 1900, BFR left England for Cape Town by ship. He was assigned to write dispatches on any war related matter and then wire these back to Pearson's office in London. On 4 April, BFR dispatched the first of thirteen such reports that was entitled *Capetown for Empire* (published 4 May 1900). Meanwhile, ACD was working as a volunteer surgeon at The Langman Hospital at Bloemfontein in South Africa.

On the 11 July 1900, both BFR and ACD departed Cape Town for England aboard a steamship called the *S.S. Briton* (see Plate 29). The pair shared a dining table and they were photographed together shortly before the ship docked at Southampton on 28 July (see Plate 30). ACD wrote in his autobiography that it was during this voyage that he 'cemented' his friendship with BFR. This statement implies that the two men had met previously, probably at the Reform Club in London to which they each belonged. ACD also recalled that during the voyage, a French Army officer called Major Roger Raoul Duval accused the British of using dum-dum bullets against the Boers. ACD reacted angrily to this allegation and BFR helped to reconcile their dispute. BFR's friend, Harold Gaye Michelmore (see Plate 31), a Devon-based solicitor and fellow 'Old Newtonian', made the following claims about that voyage in a letter that was published by *The Western Morning News* on 14 February 1949:

> …Fletcher Robinson told Doyle the plot of the story which he intended writing about Dartmoor, and Conan Doyle was so intrigued by it that he asked Fletcher Robinson if he would object to their writing it together.

> It may be interesting to recall that during the same voyage Fletcher Robinson asked Conan Doyle if it had occurred to him how easy it would be to implicate a man in a murder crime if you could

70

obtain a finger-print of his in wax for reproduction in blood on a wall or some other obvious place near the seat of the crime.

Conan Doyle was taken by the idea and asked Fletcher Robinson whether he intended to use it in his own literary work. Fletcher Robinson replied: "not immediately," and Conan Doyle offered him 50 pounds for the idea which Fletcher Robinson accepted, and Conan Doyle incorporated the idea in one of the Sherlock Holmes tales which he published shortly afterwards.

Thus it appears that BFR and ACD had agreed to co-author a Dartmoor-based story during their voyage aboard the *S.S. Briton*. However, it is unlikely that 'the story' bore much resemblance to *The Hound of the Baskervilles*. Perhaps 'the story' to which Michelmore referred is one of two other Dartmoor-linked stories that BFR wrote after the various versions of *The Hound of the Baskervilles* were published (1901/02)? The first of these is a fairy-tale entitled *The Battle of Fingle's Bridge* which was published in May 1903 by *Pearson's Magazine* (Vol. 15, pp. 530-536). The second is a short-story entitled *The Mystery of Thomas Hearne* that features as the fifth chapter of his book, *The Chronicles of Addington Peace* (June 1905). ACD used BFR's fingerprint idea in a Sherlock Holmes short story entitled *The Norwood Builder* which first appeared in *Collier's Weekly Magazine* during October 1903.

Plate 29. The *Steam Ship Briton*.
COURTESY OF THE TOPFOTO COLLECTION.

Plate 30. BFR (seated centre) and ACD
(behind his left shoulder) aboard the
*S.S. Briton* during July 1900.
THE BRIAN PUGH COLLECTION.

Plate 31. Harold Gaye Michelmore (circa 1950).

# Legendary Hounds

On 26 May 1900, the *Daily Express* published BFR's eighth dispatch under the title *Behind the Veil*. This article describes a chance encounter between BFR and a train engine driver called Richard Booth. BFR wrote that Booth was originally from Newton Abbot 'near which town I also live, we fraternalised with much hand shaking'. Hence it seems likely that BFR returned to Ipplepen shortly after his return to England on 28 July 1900. The following month, the Devonshire Association held its annual meeting at Totnes (five miles from Ipplepen). During that meeting, the *17$^{th}$ Report of the Committee on Devonshire Folk-Lore* was presented to the assembled membership. Later that same year, this report was published in the *Report and Transactions of the Devonshire Association* (Vol. XXXII, pp. 83-84). Given that Joseph Fletcher Robinson was a member of the Devonshire Association (1884-1903), it also seems likely that BFR read the following entry in that periodical:

*Wish or Yeth Hounds.* – Mr. Hardinge F. Giffard sends a valuable addition to our scanty information respecting the belief in these weird Dartmoor spectres. The late Mr. R. J. King, in an article on Dartmoor, writing of Wistman's Wood, remarked-

The name of the wood connects it with the form in which the widely-held belief in the 'wild hunter' is known on Dartmoor. The cry of the *whish* or *whished* hounds is heard occasionally in the loneliest recesses of the hills, whilst neither dogs nor huntsmen are anywhere visible. At other times (generally on a Sunday) they show themselves jet-black, breathing flames, and followed by a tall, swart figure, who carries a hunting pole. Wisc or Wish, according to Kemble, was a name of Woden, the lord of 'wish,' who is probably represented by the master of these dogs of darkness."- Quarterly Review, July, 1873.

Mr. Hardinge Giffard writes: "In 1886 or 1887, while staying for a few days in the parish of Hittisleigh (a hilly parish of scattered houses, about 8 miles W.S.W. of Crediton in Devon), I met an elderly man, whose name was, I think, Hill, from whom I endeavored to elicit some information concerning the pixies. Reluctant at first to speak on the subject, Mr. Hill, having apparently satisfied himself that my interest was genuine, told me that his father, who had died a very old man, firmly believed in the existence of the wish or yeth hounds. This belief was based on his experience, which, as told by his son, was as follows. Mr. Hill, senior, was at one time employed at the stables at Oaklands, Okehampton, now the property of

General Holley. Late one evening, when the horses had been groomed by himself and others, he heard what he believed to be a pack of hounds in full cry at no great distance. Leaving the stables, Mr. Hill ran out and distinctly heard the sound of a horn and the cry of hounds on the moor (Dartmoor) close at hand. Astonished and frightened, he returned to the stables, only to find the horses, which he had left cool and comfortable, trembling with fear and covered with sweat. My informant assured me that his father swore to the truth of his statement, and ever afterwards was a firm believer in the wish hounds, which are popularly supposed to haunt the vicinity of Dartmoor on certain nights in the year, more especially on St. John's Eve [23rd June]. Without actually admitting it in so many words, my informant obviously inherited his father's belief. I should add that Mr. Hill assured me that it was established beyond doubt that no pack of hounds in the flesh had been anywhere in the neighbourhood on the night in question." H.F.G.

Those that have read *The Hound of the Baskervilles* will note parallels between the above tale and the 'Baskerville Legend' that is communicated to Sherlock Holmes by Mortimer. The reference to Woden, the English Anglo-Saxon God of wisdom is particularly striking because he is frequently portrayed in folklore as the leader of a 'Wild Hunt' (see Plate 32). Such myths entail a mad pursuit across the sky by phantasmal huntsmen with horses and hounds. In many Scandinavian and German versions, the hunt is often for a woman, who is captured or killed. It is notable that in the 'Baskerville Legend', a Yeoman's daughter dies of fear and fatigue after fleeing across Dartmoor from a pack of hunting hounds that is led by her kidnapper, the 'wicked Hugo Baskerville'. Significantly Woden is also known by many other names including 'Grim'. This name was integrated into the fictitious settings of 'Grimpen' and the 'great Grimpen Mire' in *The Hound of the Baskervilles*.

Plate 32. *Åsgårdsreien* (or 'Wild Hunt')
by Peter Nicolai Arbo (1872).

It appears that on Thursday 25 April 1901, BFR dined at the home of his friend and former editor, Max Pemberton (see Plate 33). At that time, thirty-seven year old Pemberton was working as an author and residing with his wife and family at 56 Fitzjohn's Avenue, Hampstead. During dinner, Pemberton told a story about a large, solitary hound, with glowing eyes that reportedly terrorised the coastline of Norfolk. In some tales, this hound, called Black Shuck (see Plate 34), would ascend from the beach at Cromer to nearby Cromer Hall on a path that took it past the Royal Links Hotel. On 25 May 1939, the London *Evening News* published the following account of Sir Max Pemberton's recollection of that dinner with BFR:

> The late Fletcher Robinson who collaborated with Doyle in the story, was dining at my house in Hampstead one night when the talk turned upon phantom dogs. I told my friend of a certain Jimmy Farman, a Norfolk marshman, who swore that there was a phantom dog on the marshes near St. Olives [near Great Yarmouth, Norfolk] and that his bitch

had met the brute more than once and had been terrified by it. 'A Great black dog it were,' Jimmy said, 'and the eyes of 'un was like railway lamps. He crossed my path down there by the far dyke and the old bitch a'most went mad wi' fear...Now surely that bitch saw a' summat I didn't see...'

Fletcher Robinson assured me that dozens of people on the outskirts of Dartmoor had seen a phantom hound and that to doubt its existence would be a local heresy. In both instances, the brute was a huge retriever, coal black and with eyes which shone like fire.

Fletcher Robinson was always a little psychic and he had a warm regard for this apparition; indeed, he expressed some surprise that no romancer had yet written about it. Three nights afterwards, Fletcher Robinson was dining with Sir [sic] Arthur. The talk at my house was still fresh in his mind and he told Doyle what I had said, emphasising that this particular marshman was as sure of the existence of the phantom hound as he was of his own being. Finally, Fletcher Robinson said 'Let us write the story together.' And to his great content Sir [sic] Arthur cordially assented."

The above description of Black Shuck resonates with the description of the hound in *The Hound of the Baskervilles*. For example, both spectres are 'coal-black' in colour and brutish in demeanour. Moreover, Black Shuck has eyes 'which shine like fire' whilst those of the hound 'glowed with a smouldering glare'. It is of course possible that Sir Max Pemberton's account of Black Shuck was influenced by having read *The Hound of the Baskervilles*. However, it is equally possible that ACD's hell-hound was shaped by Pemberton's story as retold to him by BFR. Eitherway, Black Shuck remains a strong candidate for the 'country legend that set Doyle's imagination on fire' and led to his 'supreme adventure' (see below).

Plate 33.  Max Pemberton (circa 1905).

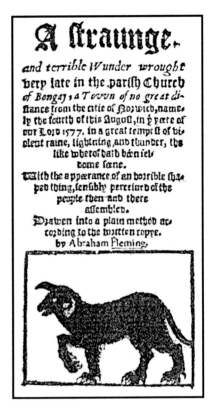

Plate 34.  Black Shuck by Abraham Fleming (1577).

# 'A Real Creeper'

Between Friday 26 April and Monday 29 April 1901, BFR and ACD stayed at the Royal Links Hotel in Cromer (see Plate 35). ACD hoped that this golfing weekend might speed his recovery from an illness that he had contracted in South Africa. However, it is unlikely that the two men played much golf that weekend because weather records reveal that it was generally overcast, damp, cold and breezy (the mean daily temperature and wind-speed were 7°C and 20.7mph). Instead, it appears that BFR entertained ACD with tales of the 'Wild Hunt' on Dartmoor and Black Shuck in Norfolk. During April 1902, a journalist called John Earnest Hodder-Williams wrote the following account of this trip to Cromer for the British version of a periodical called *The Bookman*:

> Robinson is a Devonshire man [sic], and he mentioned in conversation some old-country legend which set Doyle's imagination on fire. The two men began building up a chain of events, and in a very few hours the plot for a sensational story was conceived and it was agreed that Doyle should write it.

On Sunday 28 April, ACD sent a letter to his mother from Cromer in which, he stated that "Fletcher Robinson came here with me and we are going to do a small book together 'The Hound of the Baskervilles' – a real creeper." He also wrote a second letter to Herbert Greenhough Smith (see Plate 36), the editor of *The Strand Magazine*, in which he again described the story as a 'real creeper'. ACD offered Greenhough Smith the story but insisted that, 'I must do it with my friend Robinson and his name must appear with mine'. He added, 'I shall want my usual 50 pounds per thousand words for all rights if you do business'.

Plate 35. The clubhouse of the
Royal Links Golf Club (circa 1894).

Plate 36. Herbert Greenhough Smith.

During early May 1901, ACD decided that the book needed
some masterful central figure and reflected, 'Why should I
invent such a character when I have him already in the form of
Sherlock Holmes?' ACD subsequently contacted Greenhough
Smith and offered him a second version of the same novel, a
version that would incorporate Holmes. Greenhough Smith
agreed to pay £100 per thousand words to ACD for the Holmes
version.

# The Hound Narrative

By mid-May 1901, the first instalment of *The Hound of the Baskervilles* (Chapters I-II of XV) had arrived at the offices of *The Strand Magazine*. Records made by Sidney Paget reveal that he was paid £34 13s. at the end of May 1901 for producing seven illustrations to accompany this first instalment. This would have been impossible if Paget had not first read the instalment earlier that same month. On Saturday 25 May 1901, the following announcement appeared in *Tit-Bits*:

## The Revival of Sherlock Holmes

Very many readers of The Strand Magazine have asked us over and over again if we could not induce Mr. Conan Doyle to give us some more stories of this wonderful character. Mr. Conan Doyle has been engaged on other work, but presently he will give us an important story to appear in the Strand, in which the great Sherlock Holmes is the principle character. It will appear in both the British and American editions. In America the play founded upon the career of the great detective has run for many months with enormous success. It is going to be produced in London in about three months, and at the same time the new Sherlock Holmes story will commence in the Strand. It will be published as a serial of from 30,000 to 50,000 words, and the plot is one of the most interesting and striking that have [sic] ever been put before us. We are sure that all those readers of the Strand who have written to us on the matter, and those who have not, will be very glad that Mr. Conan Doyle is going to give us some more about our old favourite [sic].

Evidently, BFR was content for the story to be published under ACD's name alone because he willingly undertook two related research trips to Dartmoor during May 1901. The first of these took place in the company of his friend, the Revd Robert Duins Cooke (see Plate 37). He was the vicar of St. Andrew's Church in Ipplepen where Joseph Fletcher Robinson had been acting as churchwarden for eighteen years. In a letter published on the 9 February 1949 by *The Western Morning News*, the Revd Henry Robert Cooke reported the following:

> Sir – May I add to Mr. H. G. Michelmore's interesting letter on "The Hound of the Baskervilles." My father – Prebendary R. D. Cooke – was Vicar of Ipplepen at the date you mention, 1901. He was a great authority on Dartmoor. Mr. B. F. Robinson asked his advice and help in planning the background of his story.
>
> My father and Mr. Robinson went up to the Moor together, and under my father's guidance the details of the background were filled in on the spot! My father was very proud of this and often told his children how he had helped to write a very well known book.
>
> My sister, Mrs. Graeme, of Shaldon, has a copy of the book presented to my father by Mr. B. F. Robinson, and inscribed: "To Rev. R. D. Cooke from the assistant plot producer, Bertram Fletcher Robinson."

Between Friday 31 May and Sunday 2 June 1901, BFR made a second research trip to Dartmoor in the company of ACD. The two men stayed at the Duchy Hotel in Princetown (see page 120). It was owned by fifty-two year old Aaron Rowe (see Plate 38), and staffed by three of his daughters and two of his sisters. ACD and BFR were accompanied on this trip by Joseph Fletcher Robinson's coachman, thirty year old Henry Matthews Baskerville (see Plate 39). 'Harry' shared the same Christian and surname as a central character within the story of *The Hound of the Baskervilles*.

Plate 37. The Revd R. D. Cooke (circa 1936).
COURTESY OF FIONA MUDDEMAN.

Plate 38. Aaron Rowe (circa 1900).

On Saturday 1 June 1901, ACD wrote a letter to his mother from the Duchy Hotel (see below). This letter is important for two reasons. Firstly, it records his initial impression to the area about Princetown. Secondly, it states that he intended to visit the Robinson family home in Ipplepen. Other sources confirm that ACD did indeed play in all the cricket matches as listed. Hence, there is little reason to doubt that he also made the proposed journey to Ipplepen. At that time, the most direct route between Princetown and Ipplepen was a four hour drive that encompassed Hexworthy, Holne, Buckfastleigh, Ashburton and Denbury. This meant that ACD must have departed Devon on either the evening of 2 June or during the morning of 3 June.

Dearest of Mams

Here I am in the highest town in England. Robinson and I are exploring the moor together over our Sherlock Holmes book. I think it will work splendidly – indeed I have already done nearly half of it. Holmes is at his very best, and it is a highly dramatic idea which I owe to Robinson.

We did 14 miles over the Moor today and we are now pleasantly weary. It is a great place, very sad & wild, dotted with the dwellings of prehistoric man, strange monoliths and huts and graves. In those old days there was evidently a population of very many thousands here & now you may walk all day and never see one human being. Everywhere there are gutted tin mines. Tomorrow we drive 16 miles to Ipplepen where R's parents live. Then on Monday Sherborne for the cricket, 2 days at Bath, 2 days at Cheltenham. Home on Monday 10th. That is my programme.

A trip to Buckfastleigh would have enabled BFR to show ACD both the former home and possible grave of Squire Richard Cabell III (see Chapter 5). An entry in *The House of Commons Journal* for 1647 reports that he was fined by Parliament for siding with the Royalists during the English Civil War. Later, he retracted his support for King Charles I and was pardoned. Undoubtedly, this act angered local people who depended upon The Duchy of Cornwall for their livelihood. Perhaps for this reason, malicious stories about the Squire abounded. In one such story, he reputedly accused his wife of adultery and a struggle ensued. She fled to nearby Dartmoor but he recaptured and murdered her with his hunting knife. The victim's pet hound exacted revenge by ripping out the Squire's throat and some say that its anguished howls can still be heard at night. In reality, Cabell's wife actually outlived her husband by fourteen years but the legend nevertheless persisted. Again, there are parallels between this story and the legend of the 'wicked Hugo Baskerville' in *The Hound of the Baskervilles*. Later, Holmes solved the case when he noticed a resemblance between a 1647 portrait of Hugo dressed as a Royalist and another character called Stapleton. It is possible that this part of the 'Baskerville Legend' was suggested by BFR, who was interested in Devon folklore and also held a history degree.

Plate 39. Henry Baskerville (coachman).

On 26 November 1905, a Californian born journalist called Henry Jackson Wells Dam published an article entitled *Arthur Conan Doyle – An Appreciation of the Author of 'Sir Nigel', the Great Romance Which Begins Next Sunday*, in the *Sunday Magazine* supplement of *The New York Tribune*. This article included an account of BFR's recollections about his trip to Dartmoor with ACD:

> One of the most interesting weeks that I have ever spent was with Doyle on Dartmoor. He made the journey in my company shortly after I told him, and he had accepted from me, a plot which eventuated in the 'Hound of the Baskervilles'. Dartmoor, the great wilderness of bog and rock that cuts Devonshire at this point, appealed to his imagination. He listened eagerly to my stories of ghost hounds, of the headless riders and of the devils that lurk in the hollows – legends upon which I have been reared, for my home lay on the boarders of the moor. How well he turned to account his impressions will be remembered by all readers of 'The Hound'.

> Two incidents come especially to my recollection. In the centre of the moor lies the famous convict prison of Princetown. In the great granite buildings, swept by the rains and clouded in the mists, are lodged over a thousand criminals, convicted on the more serious offences. A tiny village clusters at the foot of the slope on which they stand, and a comfortable old-fashioned inn affords accommodation to travellers.

> The morning after our arrival Doyle and I were sitting in the smoking-room when a cherry-cheeked maid opened the door and announced 'Visitors to see you, gentlemen' [probably one of Aaron Rowe's daughters]. In marched four men, who solemnly sat down and began to talk about the weather, the fishing in the moor streams and other general subjects. Who they might be I had not the slightest idea. As they left I followed

them into the hall of the inn. On the table were their four cards. The governor of the prison, the deputy governor, the chaplain and the doctor had come [William Russell, Cyril Platt, Lawrence Hudson and William Frew respectively], as a pencil note explained, 'to call on Mr. Sherlock Holmes.'

One morning I took Doyle to see the mighty bog, a thousand acres of quaking slime, at any part of which a horse and rider might disappear, which figured so prominently in *The Hound*. He was amused at the story I told him of the moor man who on one occasion saw a hat near the edge of the morass and poked at it with a long pole he carried. 'You leave my hat alone!' came a voice from beneath it. 'Whoi'! Be there a man under 'at?' cried the startled rustic. 'Yes, you fool, and a horse under the man.'

From the bog we tramped eastward to the stone fort of Grimspound, which the savages of the Stone Age in Britain, the aborigines who were earlier settlers than Saxons or Danes or Norsemen, raised with enormous labour to act as a haven of refuge from marauding tribes to the South. The good preservation in which the Grimspound fort still remains is marvellous. The twenty-feet slabs of granite – how they were ever hauled to their places is a mystery to historian and engineer – still encircle the stone huts where the tribe lived. Into one of these Doyle and I walked, and sitting down on the stone which probably served the three thousand year-old chief as a bed we talked of the races of the past. It was one of the loneliest spots in Great Britain. No road came within a long distance of the place. Strange legends of lights and figures are told concerning it. Add thereto that it was a gloomy day overcast with heavy cloud.

Suddenly we heard a boot strike against a stone without and rose together. It was only a lonely tourist on a walking excursion, but at sight of our heads suddenly emerging from the hut he let out a yell and bolted. Our subsequent disappearance was due to the fact that we both sat down and rocked with laughter, and as he did not return I have small doubt Mr. Doyle and I added yet another proof of the supernatural to tellers of ghost stories concerning Dartmoor...

Evidently, these experiences impressed ACD because he subsequently incorporated a bog called 'the great Grimpen Mire' and an ancient stone hut into the plot of *The Hound of the Baskervilles*. Furthermore, on Thursday 13 June 1901, less than two weeks after he met the four senior officials from Dartmoor Prison, two convicts called William Silvester and Fergus Frith made a widely publicised escape from that institution. At about that same time, ACD was completing the third instalment of *The Hound of the Baskervilles* (Chapters V-VI of XV) and he introduced a character called Selden, a fugitive from 'the great convict prison of Princetown'.

On 17 June 1901, the proof for the second instalment of *The Hound of the Baskervilles* (Chapters III-IV of XV) was returned to ACD and he then informed the editor of *The Strand Magazine* that the third instalment (Chapters V-VI of XV) was nearly finished. At the end of June 1901, ACD sent the fourth and fifth instalments (Chapters VII-IX of XV) to *The Strand Magazine*.

In mid-July 1901, ACD went on holiday to the Esplanade Hotel in Southsea, having recently submitted the sixth and seventh instalments of *The Hound of the Baskervilles* (Chapters X-XII of XV). Indeed, ACD sent corrections to *The Strand Magazine* from Southsea. During August 1901, the first of nine monthly instalments of *The Hound of the Baskervilles* appeared in the British edition of *The Strand Magazine* (see Plate 40). BFR's contribution was acknowledged in a brief footnote to Chapter I as follows:

This story owes its inception to my friend, Mr.
Fletcher Robinson, who has helped me both in the
general plot and in the local details. — A.C.D.

In September 1901, the first of nine monthly instalments of *The
Hound of the Baskervilles* appeared in the American edition of
*The Strand Magazine.*  During this same month, ACD also
completed writing the final two instalments (Chapters XIII-XV)
at his home called Undershaw, Hindhead, Surrey.  By this time
the story had increased in length to some 60,000 words meaning
that ACD was due to be paid £6,000 for the serialisation.
Entries in ACD's account book for 1901 reveal that he paid
BFR over £500 before the end of that year.

Plate 40. *The Strand Magazine* (August 1901).

Plate 41. The cover of the
first British book edition.

On Tuesday 25 March 1902, *The Hound of the Baskervilles* was
published as a novel by George Newnes Limited of London (see
Plate 41). It preceded by one month the publication of the final
episode in the British edition of *The Strand Magazine*. The
British book edition carries the following acknowledgement:

*MY DEAR ROBINSON,*

*It was to your account of a West-Country legend that
this tale owes its inception. For this and for your
help in the details all thanks.*

*Yours most truly,*

*A. CONAN DOYLE.*

HINDHEAD,
HASLEMERE.

Thereafter, BFR gave first British book editions of *The Hound
of the Baskervilles* to 'Harry' Baskerville, the Revd Robert
Duins Cooke and his wife, Agnes Cooke. The last of these three
gifts contains a handwritten inscription in which, BFR reports
the extent of his involvement with the development of that story
(see Plate 42).

90

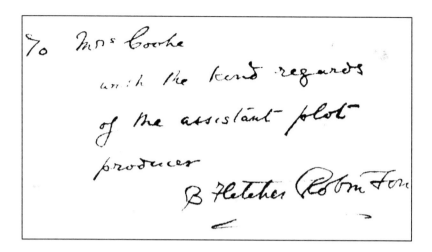

Plate 42. The inscription within the copy of the first British
book edition of *The Hound of The Baskervilles* that
was presented to Agnes Cooke by BFR.
BY COURTESY OF FIONA MUDDEMAN.

On Tuesday 15 April 1902, *The Hound of the Baskervilles* was
published as a novel by McClure, Phillips and Company (New
York). This, the first American edition of the book, includes a
version of ACD's acknowledgement letter to BFR. This version
was written, from dictation, on Sunday 26 January 1902, by
ACD' secretary, Major Charles Terry. This letter is now held
by the Berg Collection in New York Public Library and it reads:

MY DEAR ROBINSON

It was your account of a west country legend which
first suggested the idea of this little tale to my
mind. For this, and for the help which you gave
me in its evolution, all thanks. Yours most truly,
A. Conan Doyle.

The monthly sales of the British edition of *The Strand Magazine*
doubled in circulation to nearly 300,000 copies during the
serialisation of *The Hound of the Baskervilles*. The first British
book edition sold nearly 25,000 copies prior to the publication
of the final episode in that same magazine in April 1902. The

91

first American book edition sold at the rate of 5,000 copies per day for the first ten days after its publication. Moreover, this tale has since formed the basis for at least twenty-four full-length films in six different languages. Hence, it is possibly the most filmed story of all time.

## Gossip Hounds

During October 1901, shortly after the publication of the first instalment of *The Hound of the Baskervilles* in the American version of *The Strand Magazine*, the following remarks were printed in the American version of the magazine, *The Bookman*:

> Every one who read the opening chapters of the resuscitation of Sherlock Holmes in the September number of the Strand Magazine must have come to the conclusion that Dr. Doyle's share in the collaboration was a very small one. The Hound of the Baskervilles opens very dramatically, and promised to be a good tale. But the Sherlock Holmes to whom we are introduced is a totally different personage from the Sherlock Holmes of The Study in Scarlet [sic], The Sign of Four, The Adventures and The Memoirs. Of course all the little superficial tricks and mannerisms have been worked in, but there it ends. In a brief note Dr. Doyle, whose name alone is at the head of the story, acknowledges the collaboration of Mr. Fletcher Robinson. Of course the matter is one which concerns primarily only the two authors and their publishers: but we have very little hesitation in expressing our conviction that the story is almost entirely Mr. Robinson's and that Dr. Doyle's only important contribution to the partnership is the permission to use the character of Sherlock Holmes.

The American version of *The Bookman* was renowned for publishing literary gossip. This article was probably written by one of its editors called Arthur Bartlett Maurice because he later by-lined a second article that featured in the same periodical and returned to the topic of authorship. This second item was published shortly after the release of the first American book edition of *The Hound of the Baskervilles* (15 April 1902). In this later article, Maurice echoed the earlier comments, albeit in a slightly more circumspect manner:

> When the subject of this story was first discussed in literary and publishing circles in London there prevailed the idea that Mr. Fletcher Robinson had in hand a story to which Dr. Doyle was lending some assistance, his name, and the character Sherlock Holmes. A little later it was being said that Dr. Doyle and Mr. Robinson were in collaboration on this new Sherlock Holmes story. Finally, the first instalment of the tale itself appeared as being the work of Dr. Doyle alone. Allusion to Mr. Fletcher Robinson was made only in a foot-note, in which the reputed writer courteously, but rather vaguely, thanked Mr. Robinson for one or two hints and suggestions that had been of some value to him in the writing the story. Just what the meaning of all this was, just how much Mr. Robinson did contribute to the inception and the working out of *The Hound of the Baskervilles*, the reviewer is neither inclined nor prepared to say.

In June 1902, the American version of *The Bookman* published a story entitled *The Bound of the Astorbilts* by a writer called Charlton Andrews. This early parody of *The Hound of the Baskervilles* concluded with the following paragraph:

> As I gazed, from far out upon the moor there came the deep, unearthly baying of a gigantic hound. Weirdly it rose and fell in blood-curdling intensity until the inarticulate sound gradually shaped itself into this perfectly distinguishable wail: "I wonder how much of it Robinson wrote?"

This series of allegations and remarks was wholly unwarranted. BFR and ACD remained close friends after the publication of *The Hound of the Baskervilles* and they regularly associated prior to BFR's death on 21 January 1907. For example, in early 1904, ACD, BFR and Pemberton were each elected to an exclusive twelve-man criminological society referred to by its members as 'Our Society'. Indeed just two days after one of the regular meetings of 'Our Society' was held at Pemberton's house (18 October 1906), BFR and ACD played golf together in Hindhead. BFR also wrote the following relevant comment for the introduction to an item entitled *My Best Story* that appeared in the July 1905 issue of *The Novel Magazine*:

> Sir Arthur Conan Doyle is a type of the strong, clear-headed, generous Englishman, a very contrast to all that appertains to decadence. Yet there are many horrors in 'Sherlock Holmes'. It was from assisting him in 'The Hound of the Baskervilles' that I obtained my first lesson in the art of story construction. Imagination without that art is poor enough.

Consequently, any suggestion that BFR was less than perfectly content with the outcome of his literary collaboration with ACD must be dismissed. Indeed there is much evidence to support the view that BFR profited directly from his association with ACD. For example, several British and American periodicals ran serialisations of BFR's stories and these were frequently accompanied by an editorial comment that emphasised his involvement with *The Hound of the Baskervilles*. It appears that ACD was content for BFR's work to be marketed in such a way because there are no records to the contrary. This too signals the enduring respect and friendship that persisted between these two writers.

# Due Acknowledgement

The evidence suggests that ACD and BFR had fully intended to write a Dartmoor-based story together whilst aboard the *S.S. Briton* in July 1900. The theme for this story was settled upon during a subsequent visit to Cromer in late April 1901. Shortly thereafter, ACD introduced the character of Sherlock Holmes and also wrote the first instalment for *The Hound of the Baskervilles*. During the early summer of 1901, BFR and ACD conducted research for the story together in Devon. Clearly, by this stage, the two men had agreed that ACD alone should write the narrative. However, why might BFR have declined a possible offer to act as ACD's joint author?

The answer to this question will probably never be known for sure. However, it is conceivable that BFR felt that Sherlock Holmes was ACD's intellectual property and withdrew from a full collaboration upon the introduction of this character to the story (mid-May 1901). Alternatively, BFR may have been simply too busy to engage in yet another writing project. For example, during the sixteen week period when ACD was writing the narrative for *The Hound of the Baskervilles*, BFR had fourteen items published within the *Daily Express* and *Pearson's Magazine*. Moreover, he was already committed to editing a 335 page book entitled *Ice Sports* for *The Isthmian Library* (published 19 November 1901) and to writing 25,000 words for a book entitled *Sporting Pictures* (published 23 April 1902).

BFR may also have had a number of personal reasons for not contributing directly to the narrative of *The Hound of the Baskervilles*. For example, during 1901, BFR was living with his aged uncle Sir John Robinson who was also friendly with ACD. Sir John died on 30 November 1903 and the following year his autobiography entitled *Fifty Years on Fleet Street* was published by McMillan & Company Limited. The following comment appears in the foreword to this book and it was written by Sir John's friend and former employee, Frederick Moy Thomas:

I am much indebted to Sir Arthur Conan Doyle for leave to publish his striking letter to Sir John Robinson on the subject of America and the Americans; ...and to a number of Sir John's relatives and friends for similar facilities or for valuable counsel or assistance.

These lines are important for several reasons. Firstly, they reveal that the Robinson family were still on friendly terms with ACD some three years after publication of *The Hound of the Baskervilles*. This further dispels any notion that there was a controversy over authorship as alleged within the American version of *The Bookman*. Secondly, they raise the possibility that BFR was unable to assist ACD with the narrative for *The Hound of the Baskervilles* because he was already assisting Sir John with his autobiography. Certainly, BFR was well qualified to undertake such a task because he had acquired seven years of editorial experience with *The Newtonian, The Granta, The Isthmian Library, Daily Express* and *Vanity Fair*.

Additionally, BFR commenced a courtship with Gladys Morris during 1901 that ultimately led to their marriage on 3 June 1902. Throughout this period BFR's prospective father-in-law, a retired artist called Philip Morris, was struggling to keep his young family whilst battling a chronic illness that ultimately contributed to his death (22 April 1902). It seems probable that BFR would have paid regular visits to their nearby home in order to assist Philip, Gladys and her two younger siblings in whatever way he could. Similarly, BFR must have been mindful of his own father's growing infirmity and it appears that he made frequent trips to Ipplepen prior to Joseph's death on 11 August 1903.

So it appears that for the aforementioned professional and personal reasons, BFR was content to assist ACD with the plot of *The Hound of the Baskervilles* but not its narrative. Indeed, ACD confirmed as much in June 1929 when he wrote the following statement in a preface to a collection of four Sherlock

Holmes novellas entitled *The Complete Sherlock Holmes Long Stories* (London: John Murray):

> Then came The Hound of the Baskervilles. It arose from a remark by that fine fellow, whose premature death was a loss to the world, Fletcher Robinson, that there was a spectral dog near his home on Dartmoor. That remark was the inception of the book, but I should add that the plot and every word of the actual narrative are my own.

Nevertheless, BFR is deserving of some gratitude for the role that he played in inspiring ACD to "resurrect" Sherlock Holmes who was previously "killed off" in December 1893. Following his collaboration with BFR over *The Hound of the Baskervilles*, ACD wrote a further thirty-two short stories and one novella that each feature Sherlock Holmes. However, none of these tales has eclipsed the popular success of *The Hound of the Baskervilles*. As has already been mentioned, "the supreme adventure" has formed the basis for at least twenty-four related films in six different languages and many television adaptations.

In 1912, ACD also wrote a book entitled *The Lost World* that features a character called Edward G. Malone. There are many parallels between this character and BFR. For example, both spent part of their 'boyhood' in the West Country, fished and exceeded six feet in height. Furthermore, they each became accomplished rugby players, London-based journalists and loved a woman called Gladys. Hence, the heroic character of Malone might be ACD's tribute to BFR, his former 'assistant plot producer'?

# CHAPTER FIVE

## The Arthur Conan Doyle, Sherlock Holmes and Devon Tour

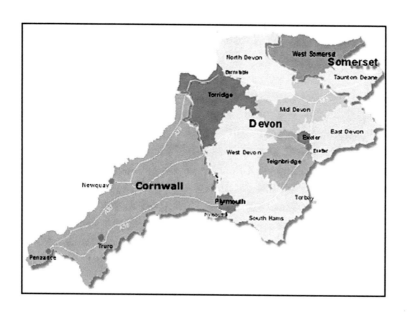

**Total Distance: 155.4 Miles**
**Total Locations: 30**
**Total Points of Interest: 56**
**Total Driving Time: 10 Hours**
**Total Walking Time: 3¼ Hours**
**Total Duration: 20 Hours**
**\* Denotes private property**

# Introduction

The Arthur Conan Doyle, Sherlock Holmes and Devon Tour is subdivided into six sections as follows: Plymouth & Roborough, Dartmoor, Newton Abbot & Ipplepen, Paignton & Torquay, Topsham & Exeter and Lynton. Readers wishing to undertake the full tour by car should allow themselves two complete days. Overnight accommodation is available at the many hotels, inns and bed & breakfast establishments that are situated on-route. Alternatively, the six subsections can be used as a basis for several inexpensive daytrips to Devon.

The authors have provided some basic maps and directions to assist readers during their tour. However, it is envisaged that some people will have little or no existing knowledge of the Devon area. Such visitors are advised to utilise *Philip's Street Atlas of Devon* (ISBN-13: 9780540081318) or GPS navigational aids (full addresses and postcodes for each location are given). Alternatively, visitors can acquire maps in advance from online resources such as *AA Route Master* or *Google Maps Latitude, Longitude Popup*. It is also worth tuning into *BBC Radio Devon* for the regular weather reports and travel bulletins both before and during the tour (103.4 & 95.7 FM).

For refreshments during the tour, the authors recommend the following; Strand Tea Rooms (24 New Street, The Barbican, Plymouth), Valentis Cafe Bar (The Promenade, The Hoe, Plymouth), The Lopes Arms (Tavistock Road, Roborough), Fox Tor Cafe (Two Bridges Road, Princetown), The Forest Inn (Hexworthy), The Old Coffee House Tea Rooms (West Street, Ashburton), Queens Hotel (Queen Street, Newton Abbot), Compass Bar and Lounge (The Grand Hotel, Torbay Road, Torquay), Langtry's Restaurant (Osborne Hotel, 2 Hesketh Crescent, Torquay) and The Oak Room (14 Lee Road, Lynton).

# Section 1
# Plymouth & Roborough

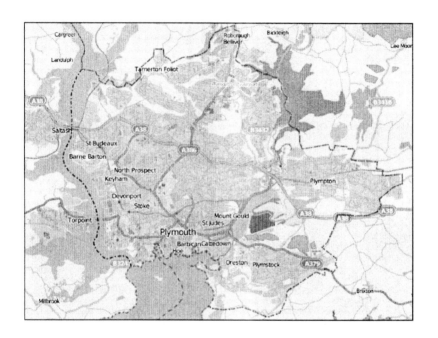

**Distance: 11.4 Miles**
**Locations: 5**
**Points of Interest: 9**
**Driving Time: 50 Minutes**
**Walking Time: 45 Minutes**
**Duration: 3½ Hours**

# Location 1
# (0 miles)

## *6 Elliot Terrace

**Hoe**
**Plymouth**
**PL1 2PL**

**Latitude: 50.365471**
**Longitude: -4.145382**

Plate 43.  Elliot Terrace (right) and the Grand Hotel
(centre) as they appeared prior to WWII.
THE BRIAN PUGH COLLECTION.

# Directions to
# Location 1

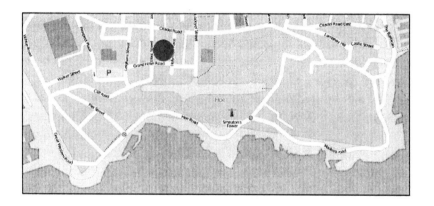

Locate Plymouth Barbican. Continue along Madeira Road that runs parallel to the walls of the Royal Citadel and seafront. At the first mini-roundabout, take the second exit for Hoe Road and park in any available pay-and-display bay located on the right. Cross the road and enter The Promenade by way of the disabled car park. Walk due west for 0.3 of a mile along The Promenade between Smeaton's Lighthouse Tower and the War Memorials. Elliot Terrace and the Grand Hotel are both located on the right (see Plate 43).

# Notes on Location 1

Elliot Terrace is a row of seven imposing six-storey Victorian mansions, constructed in around 1873 by Messrs Call & Pethick (John Pethick was the Lord Mayor of Plymouth between 1898 and 1900). The name derives from one Colonel James Elliot who once owned most of the land upon which Plymouth Hoe now stands. ACD resided with GTB and his family at number 6 Elliot Terrace following his arrival at Plymouth in around early May 1882. Later, ACD recalled that the property was largely unfurnished and that he was provided with nails upon which to hang his clothes. GTB was content to allow ACD to think that he was the sole tenant of the property, presumably in order to impress him. However, records now reveal that GTB co-leased this property with the Royal Western Yacht Club and the Grand Hotel. Clearly neither the Yacht Club nor Grand Hotel was using 6 Elliot Terrace whilst ACD resided there. It therefore seems probable that the old Grand Hotel vacated Elliot Terrace in around 1880 in order to occupy an adjacent building that was newly built by John Pethick. ACD resided at the new Grand Hotel on 22 February 1923.

Visitors might be interested to learn that 3 Elliot Terrace was bought by Waldorf Astor in 1908 (2nd Viscount Astor from 18 October 1919). On 1 December 1919 his wife, Lady Nancy Astor, became the first woman Member of Parliament to take up a seat in the House of Commons (Unionist Party). She is reported to have told Winston Churchill: "if you were my husband, I'd put arsenic in your coffee", to which he retorted, "Madam, if I were your husband, I'd drink it!" Lady Astor died on 2 May 1964 and bequeathed 3 Elliot Terrace to the City of Plymouth. This property is now the official residence of the Lord Mayor of Plymouth and it is also used to accommodate visiting dignitaries and circuit judges.

# Location 2
# (1.4 miles)

# *1 Durnford Street

**East Stonehouse**
**Plymouth**
**PL1 3QL**

**Latitude: 50.367194**
**Longitude: -4.162029**

Plate 44. 1 Durnford Street (circa 1920). The
site of this former property is now located
at the entrance to 35 Durnford Street.
THE BRIAN PUGH COLLECTION.

# Directions to
# Location 2

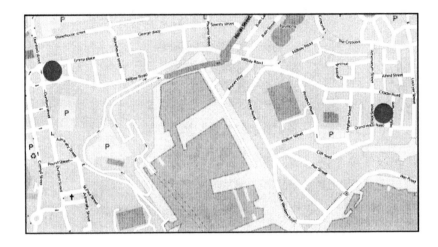

From Hoe Road, double back to the mini-roundabout off Madeira Road and then turn right towards Plymouth Dome. Continue for 0.8 of a mile along Hoe Road, Grand Parade, Great Western Road and West Hoe Road. At the roundabout, turn left towards the Continental Ferryport (Millbay Road) and continue for 0.6 of a mile. At the crossroads, keep to the right lane and park for free immediately after this junction outside numbers 12-24 Barrack Place (note that parking restrictions apply during the summer months between 10.00am and 5.00pm).

# Notes on Location 2

Durnford Street was constructed in around 1773 to provide accommodation for senior naval and military personal. During June 1881, GTB opened a surgery on the north-eastern side of the crossroads between Durnford Street and Barrack Place (see Plate 44). In around May 1882, GTB and ACD entered into partnership at this practice but the arrangement was dissolved after only seven-weeks. The former surgery and neighbouring buildings were demolished during 1958. The cleared land was later redeveloped and used to site a car dealership called Renwick's Garage. Most recently, the site of the former surgery has been incorporated into a luxury apartment block called Evolution Cove.

Until 2003, the former site of 1 Durnford Street was marked by a commemorative plaque (see Plate 15). A series of twenty-two other plaques featuring quotes from Sherlock Holmes stories can still be seen set within the footpath between 85 and 125 Durnford Street (see Plate 45). An additional plaque is mounted within the lower step at the entrance to 93 Durnford Street and it reads:

**SIR ARTHUR CONAN DOYLE**
**1859 – 1930**

IN 1882 CONAN DOYLE PRACTISED MEDICINE AT NO 1 DURNFORD STREET.
UNFORTUNATELY THE RELATIONSHIP
WITH HIS PRACTICE PARTNER WAS AN UNHAPPY ONE AND ENDED WITH CONAN
DOYLE MOVING TO SOUTHSEA.
DURING HIS SPARE TIME FROM HIS MEDICAL PROFESSION HE BECAME MORE
INVOLVED IN HIS WRITINGS. 'A STUDY
OF SCARLET', THE FIRST OF 68 STORIES FEATURING SHERLOCK HOLMES,
APPEARED IN 1887. CONAN DOYLES TIME IN
DEVON UNDOUBTEDLY INSPIRED HIS LATER LITERARY WORK, 'THE HOUND OF
THE BASKERVILLES.' A HOLMES
CULT AROSE AND STILL FLOURISHES TODAY.

This inscription contains a number of factual errors. 'A Study of Scarlet' should read 'A Study in Scarlet'; furthermore, it is generally accepted that ACD wrote sixty Sherlock Holmes stories and that his time in Durnford Street did not inspire *The Hound of the Baskervilles*. However, it is worth noting that in that story Sherlock Holmes does refer to a newspaper called the *Western Morning News*. ACD almost certainly read a regional newspaper called *The Western Morning News* during his residence in East Stonehouse.

Plate 45. A brass plaque set within the pavement at Durnford Street. The inscription reads 'Now, Watson, the fair sex is your department.' This comment is directed by Sherlock Holmes to Dr Watson in *The Adventure of the Second Stain* (December 1904).

# Location 3
# (3.1 miles)

## Plymouth Guildhall

### Guildhall Square
### Plymouth
### PL1 2AD

### Latitude: 50.369804
### Longitude: -4.141738

Plate 46. A postcard showing the northern façade
of Plymouth Guildhall (right) prior to WWII.
THE BRIAN PUGH COLLECTION.

# Directions to
# Location 3

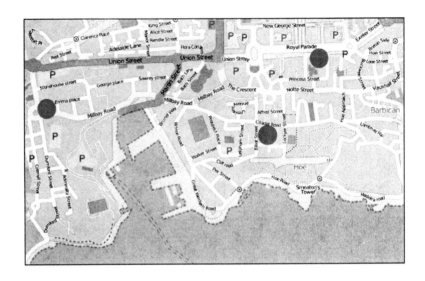

From Barrack Place, follow the one-way system for 0.2 of a mile to a roundabout and then turn right into Edgcumbe Street (signposted A38). Continue along the A374 for 0.6 of a mile to the crossroads between Union Street and The Crescent. Continue for 0.2 of a mile to Derrys Cross Roundabout and then double back towards the crossroads between Union Street and The Crescent. Just before this crossroads, turn left into The Crescent and continue for 0.3 of a mile to the fourth set of traffic lights. At these traffic lights, turn left into Princess Way, and then take the first right into Athenaeum Place. Continue for 0.1 of a mile and then turn left by Plymouth Crown and County Courts. A little further-on you will come to the Guildhall Pay and Display Car Park. Visitors may enter the Guildhall reception area and request a free tour of this building (see Plate 46).

# Notes on Location 3

In 1909, ACD met journalist Edmund Morel, who had co-founded the Congo Reform Association during 1904. The CRA wanted to publicise recent oppression of the Congolese population by the former Belgian colonists. During October 1909, ACD had a pamphlet published that was entitled *The Crime of the Congo* (Hutchinson & Co.). In the preface to this work ACD wrote: 'There are many of us in England who consider the crime which has been wrought in the Congo lands by King Leopold of Belgium and his followers to be the greatest which has ever been known in human annals.' Thereafter ACD embarked upon a three month lecture tour with Edmund Morel to promote agitation against Belgian oppression in the Congo. On 18 November 1909, they visited Plymouth Guildhall and ACD delivered a lecture entitled *The Congo Atrocity*. ACD returned there on 23 February 1923, to deliver a lecture on Spiritualism, *The New Revelation*.

Like Elliot Terrace, the Guildhall was constructed in 1873 by John Pethick and was officially opened on 13 August 1874 by His Royal Highness Prince Edward, The Prince of Wales (who later became King Edward VII and knighted ACD). It is a fine example of so-called 'early-pointed' architecture. The original building was gutted by fire during the second night of the Plymouth Blitz (20/21 March 1941). Restoration work began in January 1953 and the layout of the original building was essentially reversed. The stage on which ACD delivered his lectures is now situated at the main entrance to the post-war Guildhall building. There is also a plaque commemorating Lord and Lady Astor by the old northern entrance to this building.

111

# Location 4
## (5.2 miles)

## Ford Park Cemetery

**Ford Park Road
Plymouth
PL4 6NT**

**Latitude: 50.382749
Longitude: -4.145508**

Plate 47. The grave of Dr George Turnavine
Budd and his only son, William. It is situated in the
south-eastern section of Ford Park Cemetery.
THE BRIAN PUGH COLLECTION.

# Directions to
# Location 4

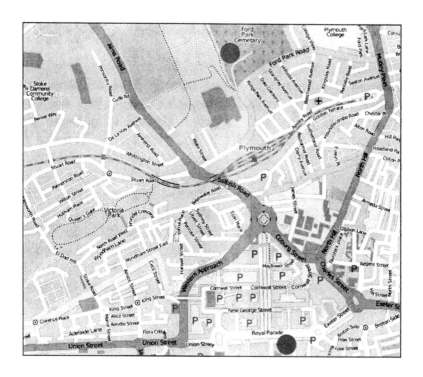

From Plymouth Guildhall, double back to the junction between Athenaeum Place and Princess Way. Turn right and follow the one-way system to Derrys Cross Roundabout. Join this roundabout and take the third exit for Royal Parade. Continue for 0.5 of a mile to Charles Cross Roundabout (site of a burned-out church). At this roundabout, take the first exit and continue for 0.3 of a mile along Charles Street and Cobourg Street towards Liskeard (A38) and Tavistock (A386). At North Cross Roundabout, take the second exit for Saltash Road and then continue for 0.3 of a mile in the right lane. At the roundabout, take the third exit for Central Park Avenue. Continue for 0.3 of a mile and then turn left into Ford Park Cemetery via the lodge-gate entrance. Visitors may park for free next to the two Victorian chapels.

# Notes on Location 4

GTB and his son, William, are buried together at Ford Park Cemetery (see Plate 47). ACD used GTB as a model for a character called Dr James Cullingworth and possibly a second character called Professor George Edward Challenger (see Chapter 2). To locate GTB's grave, walk 100 yards down the processional drive towards the lodge-gate entrance and then turn right just after the Garden of Remembrance. Continue along the tarmac path for 50 yards to the stone-steps on the right. Just beyond and to the left of these steps is the grave of Lieutenant James Arthur Reynolds (marked by a large anchor). GTB's grave is sited four rows back from this grave (Plot: CLG, 41, 4). Care should be exercised, particularly during wet weather, as the ground underfoot is slippery and can conceal items that might trip an unwary visitor!

Visitors may also wish to visit the joint grave of GTB's uncle, Dr John Wreford Budd, and his son, Robert Sutton Budd (GTB's cousin). To locate this grave from the car park, walk 40 yards down the processional drive towards the lodge-gate entrance. Take the second grass pathway on the right, then turn right again immediately before a large round tomb. The Budd grave is located on the right some four graves back and two graves in (Plot: D, 26, 17). Visitors are encouraged to enquire at the office adjacent to the new chapel and car park about the Ford Park Heritage Trail. There are many other interesting characters buried at this cemetery including the former Lord Mayor of Plymouth, John Pethick (1827-1904), who built Elliot Terrace, Plymouth Guildhall and the new Grand Hotel (Plot: CHA, 16, 2).

# Location 5
# (11.4 miles)

# The Lopes Arms

**27 Tavistock Road
Roborough
Plymouth
PL6 7BD**

**Latitude: 50.441315
Longitude: -4.108220**

Plate 48. The western façade of The Lopes Arms.
THE BRIAN PUGH COLLECTION.

# Directions to
# Location 5

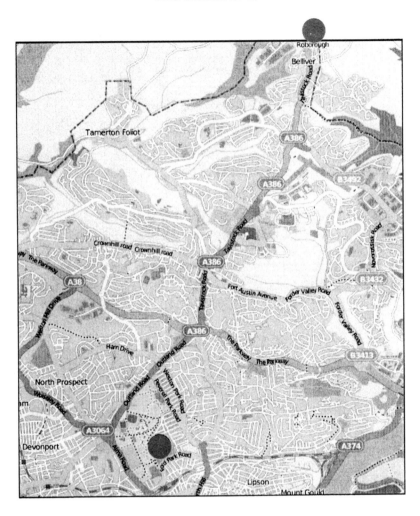

From Ford Park Cemetery, double back to the roundabout off Saltash Road. At this roundabout, take the third exit which is sign posted Saltash, Liskeard and the A38. Continue for 5.4 miles along Outland Road and Tavistock Road (A386) to the third major roundabout by Belliver Industrial Estate.

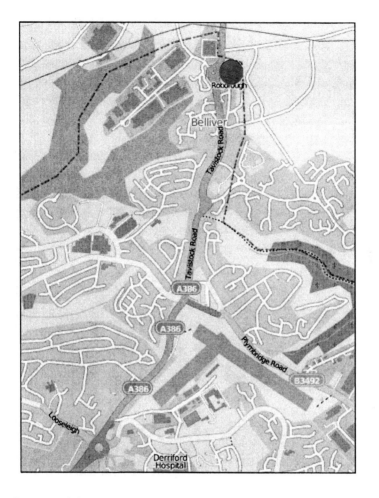

At the roundabout by Belliver Industrial Estate, take the third exit and double back along Tavistock Road towards Plymouth. After 0.2 of a mile turn left into the old Tavistock Road (sign posted Roborough). Continue for 0.2 of a mile past Leatside Walk and Leatside. The Lopes Arms (see Plate 48) is located on the right and visitors may park for free on the road outside these premises. Visitors wishing to take refreshments at the pub are also permitted to use their car parking facilities for free.

# Notes on Location 5

During June 1882, GTB and ACD dissolved their medical partnership and ACD travelled to Tavistock to investigate the possibility of opening-up his own practice there. During that trip, he visited The Lopes Arms at the boundary between Plymouth and the southern edge of Dartmoor. ACD had a semi-fictional account of a photographic expedition from Plymouth to Tavistock, *Dry Plates on a Wet Moor,* published in the *British Journal of Photography* in November 1882. In this article, ACD refers to The Lopes Arms as 'The Admiral Vernon Public House'. The same trip undoubtedly inspired the setting for a later Sherlock Holmes story, *The Adventure of Silver Blaze,* first published in *The Strand Magazine* in 1892 (see Plate 49).

Plate 49. The cover of the British edition of *The Strand Magazine* that featured *The Adventure of Silver Blaze* (December 1892).

118

# Section 2
# Dartmoor

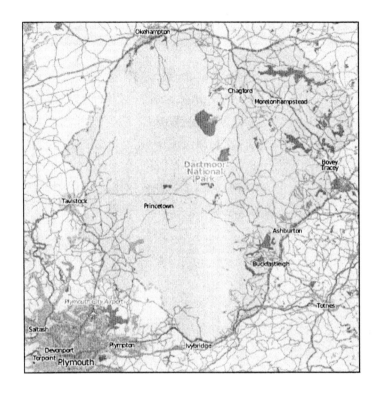

## Distance: 22.6 Miles
## Locations: 7
## Points of Interest: 14
## Driving Time: 60 Minutes
## Walking Time: 40 Minutes
## Duration: 3½ Hours

# Location 6
# (21.3 miles)

# <u>High Moorland Visitor Centre</u>

**Tavistock Road**
**Princetown**
**Yelverton**
**PL20 6QF**

**Latitude:  50.544114**
**Longitude:  -3.990800**

Plate 50.  The Duchy Hotel (circa 1905).
PHOTOGRAPH BY DAVID GERMAN.

# Directions to
# Location 6

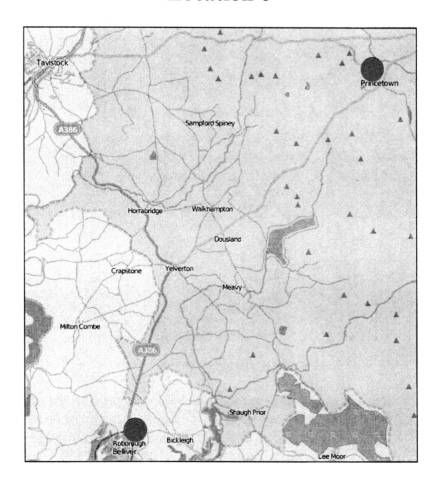

From The Lopes Arms, continue north along the old Tavistock
Road to the junction with the A386. Turn left and return to the
roundabout by Belliver Industrial Estate. At this roundabout,
take the third exit for Tavistock. Continue for 3.8 miles across
Roborough Down to the major roundabout at Yelverton. At this
roundabout, take the second exit which is sign posted
'Princetown' and the 'B3212'.

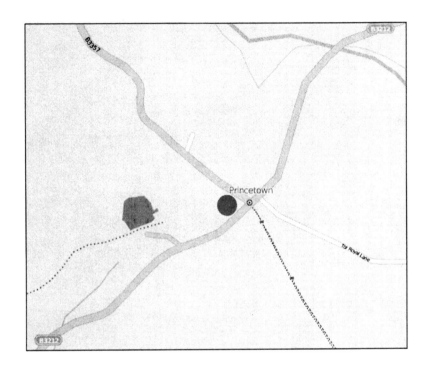

Upon reaching the mini-roundabout in Princetown, take the first exit for Tavistock Road (B3357). Continue for 100 yards and then turn left into Station Cottages Royal Court. Follow signs for the High Moorland Visitor Centre Car Park (a small fee is charged for parking).

# Notes on Location 6

The building that now houses the High Moorland Visitor Centre was constructed in around 1809 to accommodate officers of the Army and Militia who were employed to guard Napoleonic prisoners of war at what is now HM Prison Dartmoor. During 1850, Mr James Rowe acquired this property and reopened it as the Duchy Hotel (see Plate 50). He also installed a beautiful tiled mosaic in the reception area that can still be seen and reads, 'Welcome the coming, speed the parting guest' (derived from Pope's translation of Homer's Odyssey). On 2 June 1901, ACD wrote a letter to his mother from the Duchy Hotel in which he reported:

> I am in the highest town in England. Robinson [BFR] and I are exploring the Moor over our Sherlock Holmes book. I think it will work out splendidly – indeed I have already done nearly half of it. Holmes is at his very best, and is a highly dramatic idea – which I owe to Robinson...

During 1990 the Dartmoor National Park Authority began converting the former Duchy Hotel into the present day Visitor Centre, which was officially opened by His Royal Highness Prince Charles, The Prince of Wales, on 9 June 1993. Several of the original hotel signs are still visible on the exterior walls of the Visitor Centre (see Plate 51). In the centre shop visitors may view a life-size photograph of ACD and a mannequin of Sherlock Holmes (see Plate 52). The exhibit section includes further information about ACD, BFR and *The Hound of the Baskervilles* (a small donation is requested).

Plate 51. Paul R. Spiring (left) and Brian W. Pugh (right) with the actor Edward Hardwicke outside the former Duchy Hotel. The latter man played Dr Watson alongside Jeremy Brett as Sherlock Holmes in the Granada Television adaptation of *The Return of Sherlock Holmes* series (1986-1994).

Plate 52. The life-size photograph of ACD and the mannequin of Sherlock Holmes inside the Visitor Centre.

# Location 7
## (24.0 miles)

# Fox Tor Mires

**Tor Royal Lane
Whiteworks Tin Mine
Princetown
Yelverton
PL20 6SL**

**Latitude: 50.522506
Longitude: -3.958399**

Plate 53. Fox Tor Mires as seen from Peat Cot Hill. The buildings are the Whiteworks Mine Cottages (built in 1871).

# Directions to
# Location 7

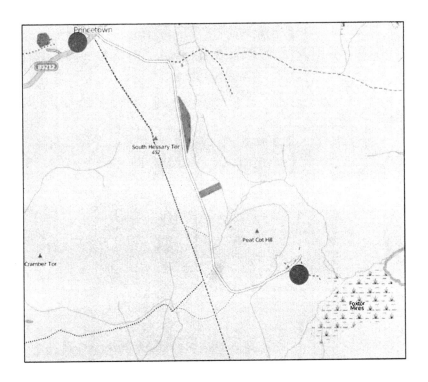

From the Visitor Centre, return to the mini-roundabout at the junction between Tavistock Road and the B3212. At this roundabout, turn left into Two Bridges Road and then turn right into Tor Royal Lane. Continue for 2.6 miles to the derelict Whiteworks Tin Mine near Peat Cot Hill. Visitors can park for free at the entrance to the derelict tin mine or opposite the Whiteworks Mine Cottages (see Plate 53).

# Notes on Location 7

The Fox Tor Mires are situated at the heart of a bowl-shaped depression between Fox Tor, Childe's Tomb and Whiteworks Tin Mine. The impermeable nature of the granite bedrock coupled with high annual rainfall means that the area is poorly drained and perpetually boggy. Fox Tor Mires is known locally as a 'feathered' mire because trampling sometimes causes the ground both underfoot and beyond to quiver.

BFR and ACD are known to have visited a bog during their research trip to Dartmoor during 1901 (see page 87). It is probable that this bog was Fox Tor Mires and that this location inspired the 'great Grimpen Mire', which is so pivotal to the plot of *The Hound of the Baskervilles*. For example, readers of that story will recall that the villain Stapleton keeps *The Hound* on a small island at the centre of the 'great Grimpen Mire' and that he apparently dies whilst attempting to escape to there. Moreover, the north-western edge of Fox Tor Mires ends inside the perimeter of the derelict Whiteworks Tin Mine. The 'great Grimpen Mire' also contains the remains of a tin mine within its boundary.

In reality, the 'great Grimpen Mire' is many more times treacherous than Fox Tor Mires. Nevertheless, it is possible to suffer the ill-effects of exposure should one become stuck waist deep in the peaty water filled hollows that line the several paths that cross the mire. For that reason, uninitiated readers wishing to explore the Fox Tor Mires further are advised to do so only in the company of an experienced local guide. More information about such guides is available from the High Moorland Visitor Centre in Princetown.

# Location 8
# (26.9 miles)

# *Her Majesty's Prison Dartmoor

**Tavistock Road**
**Princetown**
**Yelverton**
**PL20 6RR**

**Latitude: 50.547874**
**Longitude: -3.987232**

Plate 54. HM Prison Dartmoor
and North Hessary Tor.

# Directions to
# Location 8

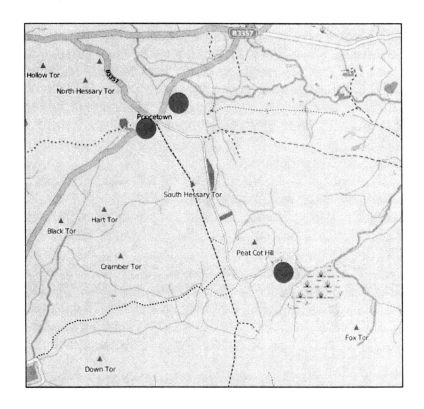

From Fox Tor Mires, double back to the junction between Tor Royal Lane and Two Bridges Road. Turn right and continue for 0.3 of a mile to a lay-by just beyond Princetown. This location provides an excellent view of Dartmoor Prison (see Plate 54).

# Notes on Location 8

Originally constructed between 1806 and 1809 to act as a depot for prisoners from the Napoleonic War (1803-1815), the prison was commissioned as a convict gaol in 1850 and has remained so ever since. During the Victorian era, Dartmoor was reputed to have the most severe régime of any British prison and it was used to incarcerate the most dangerous convicts. Visitors who wish to learn more about the history of 'Dartmoor Prison' are encouraged to visit its Heritage Centre which is located on Tavistock Road in Princetown (free car park with a small fee for entrance to the exhibit area).

Between 31 May and 2 June 1901, ACD and BFR met the governor, deputy governor, chaplain and physician of Dartmoor Prison (William Russell, Cyril Platt, Lawrence Hudson and William Frew respectively). On 13 June 1901, two convicts called William Silvester and Fergus Frith made a widely publicised escape from Dartmoor Prison. At about that same time, ACD was completing the third instalment of *The Hound of the Baskervilles* (Chapters V-VI of XV) and introduced a character called Selden, also a fugitive from Dartmoor Prison.

ACD featured Dartmoor Prison in three other stories: *The Sign of Four* (February 1890), *How the King Held the Brigadier* (April 1895) and *How the Brigadier Triumphed in England* (March 1903*)*. The first of these stories was the second Sherlock Holmes novella and the other two tales are both Brigadier Gerard stories.

# Location 9
# (38.4 miles)

# *Brook Manor

### Near Hockmoor Hill
### Buckfastleigh
### TQ11 OHR

### Latitude: 50.496027
### Longitude: -3.817147

Plate 55.  Brook Manor (southern façade).
PHOTOGRAPH BY ANTHONY HOWLETT ©1992.

# Directions to
# Location 9

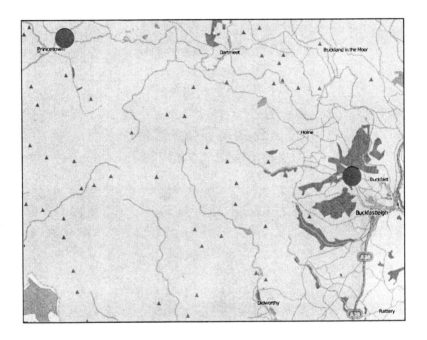

From the lay-by opposite HM Prison Dartmoor, continue for 1.0 mile to a T-junction and then turn right towards Two Bridges (B3357). Continue for 4.1 miles in the direction of Ashburton and then turn right towards Hexworthy. Continue for 4.6 miles past Venford Reservoir and towards the village of Holne. Upon entering Holne, turn right at the first sign marked Scoriton.

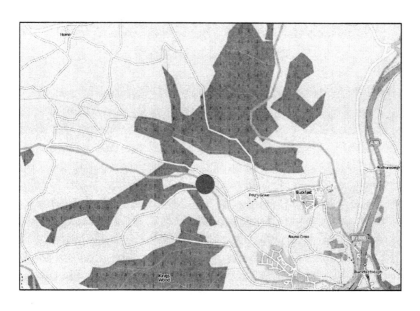

After entering Holne and turning right, continue for 0.4 of a mile and then take the second turning on the right (at the second sign for Scoriton). Continue for 1.1 miles past Littlecombe Farm and The Tradesmans Public House to a crossroads. Here, turn right towards Buckfastleigh and continue for 0.4 of a mile to a red letterbox mounted in the wall on the left. Visitors can park for free just beyond this letterbox near the entrance to Hawson Court and Stables. Opposite the letterbox is a five-bar gate from which a good view of Brook Manor (see Plate 55) may be enjoyed.

# Notes on Location 9

Brook Manor was constructed in 1656 for Squire Richard Cabell III (1622-1672). An entry in *The House of Commons Journal* for 1647 reported that Cabell was fined by Parliament for siding with the Royalists in the English Civil War. He subsequently retracted his support for King Charles 1 and was pardoned. This act no doubt angered local people who were dependent for their livelihood upon The Duchy of Cornwall Estate. Perhaps for this reason, malicious stories about this unprincipled squire abounded. For example, one night Cabell reputedly accused his wife of adultery and a struggle ensued. She fled to nearby Dartmoor but he recaptured and murdered her with his hunting knife. The victim's pet hound exacted revenge by ripping out Cabell's throat and some say that its anguished howls can still be heard. In reality, Cabell's wife actually outlived him by some fourteen years but the legend nevertheless persisted. There are parallels between this story and the legend of the wicked Hugo Baskerville that was reported to Sherlock Holmes by James Mortimer in *The Hound of the Baskervilles*. Later, Holmes solved the case when he noticed a resemblance between a 1647 portrait of Hugo Baskerville dressed as a Royalist and the villain, Stapleton.

# Location 10
# (40.3 miles)

## <u>Holy Trinity Church</u>

### Church Hill
### Buckfastleigh
### TQ11 OEZ

### Latitude: 50.485239
### Longitude: -3.774194

Plate 56.  The sepulchre built for Squire Richard
Cabell III.  It is located opposite the church porch.
THE BRIAN PUGH COLLECTION.

# Directions to
# Location 10

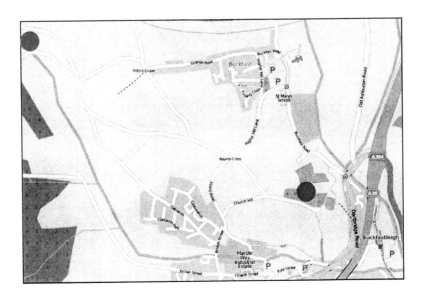

From Brook Manor, continue for 1.5 miles in the direction of Buckfastleigh to the Round Crossroads. Go straight over the crossroads and continue for 0.4 of a mile towards the tower of Holy Trinity Church. Visitors can park for free outside the main entrance to this church.

# Notes on Location 10

Holy Trinity Church is primarily a Thirteenth Century building but it has a Fifteenth Century nave. On 8 May 1849, arsonists began a fire that destroyed the vestry and the parish chest. The same fire also badly damaged the communion table and a section of the roof belonging to the northern aisle. During WWII, rogue German bombs shattered some of the stained glass windows. On 21 July 1992, arsonists again attacked the church but on this occasion the ensuing inferno completely gutted the interior of the building. Today, Holy Trinity Church stands as a near empty shell, although services are still held there intermittently during the summer months.

The evidently unpopular Squire Richard Cabell III died during the summer of 1672. His notoriety has spawned other fanciful tales, and the various misfortunes that befell Holy Trinity Church have been linked to the 'sepulchre' or 'penthouse tomb' that he had constructed there (see Plate 56). It has even been suggested that the heavy tombstone enclosed therein was intended to prevent his ghost from escaping to Dartmoor and riding to hounds. However, it is not known for sure whether Squire Richard Cabell III is actually interned within the sepulchre. The tombstone does bear the name 'Richard Cabell' (in Latin) but this might refer to either his grandfather or father who both predeceased him and were also so named. The tombstone has been damaged through past acts of vandalism or black magic rites and it is now safeguarded by an iron grill.

# Location 11
# (43.9 miles)

# St. Andrew's Church

**West Street**
**Ashburton**
**TQ13 7DT**

**Latitude: 50.513067**
**Longitude: -3.756623**

Plate 57. The grave of Henry 'Harry'
Baskerville and his wife, Alice. It is located in the
southern section of St. Andrew's Church.

# Directions to
# Location 11

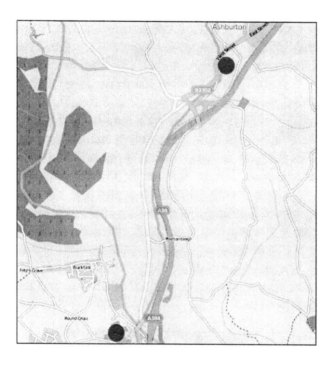

From Holy Trinity Church, double back to the Round Crossroads and turn right towards Buckfast. Continue for 0.4 of a mile to the mini-roundabout just beyond the entrance to Buckfast Abbey. Take the second exit and continue for 0.4 of a mile to a second mini-roundabout. Take the first exit for Exeter, Plymouth and Totnes. Cross the bridge that spans the River Dart and then turn left towards Ashburton and Princetown. Continue for 1.7 miles to the T-junction by Pear Tree Service Station; then turn left. Continue for 50 yards and then turn right onto Western Road that leads to both Ashburton and Buckland in the Moor (B3352). Continue for 0.5 of a mile, before turning left into Kingsbridge Lane by the public toilets. Follow signs to the pay-and-display car park. Having parked, leave the car park through the archway located in the south-western corner. Turn right (West Street) and walk 50 yards up the hill to the main entrance for St. Andrew's Church (located on the left).

# Notes on Location 11

Henry 'Harry' Baskerville is buried in the graveyard here. It will be recalled that he drove ACD and BFR about Dartmoor when the two men researched the setting for *The Hound of the Baskervilles* during 1901 (see Chapter 4). Baskerville also shared the same Christian name and surname as a major character in the book. To locate his grave (see Plate 57) enter the graveyard by way of the main gate and turn right. Walk 100 yards along the tarmac path that runs parallel to a tall stonewall. At the end of this wall, turn right onto a smaller tarmac path by the grave of Richard Bennett. Ascend the hill past twelve rows of graves and turn left at the headstone for Edward Amery Adams. The grave of Henry Baskerville and his wife, Alice (née Perring), is located seven plots in from this headstone. A second grave bearing the name of a character featured in *The Hound of the Baskervilles* is also situated nearby. To locate the grave of 'James Mortimer', return to the grave of Richard Bennett. Mortimer's grave (see Plate 58) is situated three rows up and four plots in.

Plate 58. The grave of the former local
Headmaster, James Mortimer.
THE BRIAN PUGH COLLECTION.

# Location 12
# (43.9 miles)

## *Dorncliffe

**18 West Street
Ashburton
TQ13 7DT**

**Latitude: 50.515048
Longitude: -3.756966**

Plate 59. 'Dorncliffe' was Henry
'Harry' Baskerville's final home.

# Directions to
# Location 12

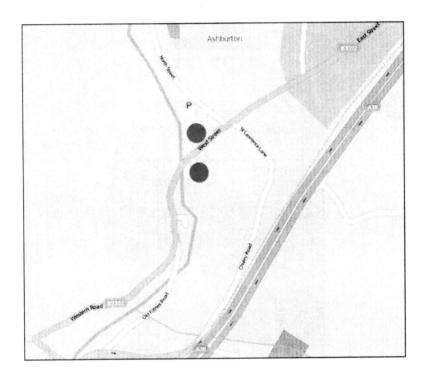

Return to the main entrance of St. Andrew's Church and turn right. Walk 50 yards to Ashburton Methodist Chapel where the funeral service for Henry 'Harry' Baskerville was held on 31 March 1962. Situated directly opposite the chapel is number 18 West Street or 'Dorncliffe' (see Plate 59).

# Notes on Location 12

Plate 60. Henry 'Harry' Baskerville (circa 1959).

Henry 'Harry' Baskerville (see Plates 40 & 60) worked for the Robinson family for some twenty years until 1905 when BFR's mother, Emily Robinson was admitted to Springfield Nursing Home in Newton Abbot. He then moved to Ashburton where he worked as a gardener for a further fifty-two years for an influential local family called Sawdye. Initially, Baskerville resided with his family in East Street (1905-1908) and then at 'Laburnums' (1909-1931). Thereafter, he resided at 18 West Street until his death in 1962 aged 91 years.

During the fifty-seven years that he lived in Ashburton, Baskerville served on the Urban District Council for eight years. He also became a member of the Court Leet and Baron Juries and was elected as the Chairman of the Co-operative Society, a post that he held for twelve years. Baskerville was also a prominent member of Ashburton Methodist Church and he had held the offices of Circuit Steward, Society Steward, Poor Steward and Trustee. On 6 February 1961, Douglas Cock interviewed Baskerville at Dorncliffe for local BBC Radio. During this interview Baskerville made the following comments relating to *The Hound of the Baskervilles*:

> ...Conan Doyle came and I fetched him from Newton Abbot Station, he remained at Park Hill for eight days and I took him back again, I also took him around Bovey Tracy and Heatree...to have a look around Hound Tor and...pick up some of the threads of the story. The book was written and they promised me the first issue...which I had...As a young man I didn't think anything about sending my copy...to Conan Doyle to have him [sic] autographed...not till after the film came out and then I thought well what a stupid [sic], I haven't sent the book to Conan Doyle...

During this short interview, Baskerville appears frequently muddled. The film to which he referred was the 1959 Hammer Films version of *The Hound of the Baskervilles*, which starred Peter Cushing as Holmes, André Morell as Dr Watson and Christopher Lee as Sir Henry Baskerville. Baskerville had enjoyed wide publicity prior to the release of this film. This observation has led some to suggest that he overstated his role and that of BFR in the inception of the story.

144

# Section 3
## Newton Abbot
## & Ipplepen

**Distance: 4.7 Miles**
**Locations: 5**
**Points of Interest: 13**
**Driving Time: 30 Minutes**
**Walking Time: 40 Minutes**
**Duration: 3 Hours**

# Location 13
# (52.2 miles)

# <u>Newton Abbot Railway Station</u>

**Station Road**
**Newton Abbot**
**TQ12 2BT**

**Latitude: 50.529962**
**Longitude: -3.599736**

Plate 61.  Newton Abbot Railway Station (1927).
©HUTTON ARCHIVE

# Directions to
# Location 13

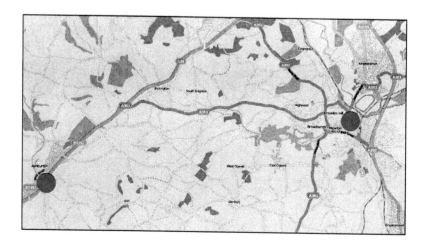

From the car park in Ashburton, follow the one-way system to North Street. Turn right and continue for 100 yards to a T-junction. Turn left into East Street (B3352) and follow all signs for Exeter, Newton Abbot and the A38. Join the Exeter bound carriageway of the A38 and continue for 0.7 of a mile. Join the A383 (sign posted Newton Abbot) and continue for 5.0 miles to the first roundabout in Newton Abbot. Take the second exit that is sign posted Town Centre, Totnes and A381. Continue for 0.3 of a mile to the traffic lights by the ASDA superstore and turn left into Halcyon Road.

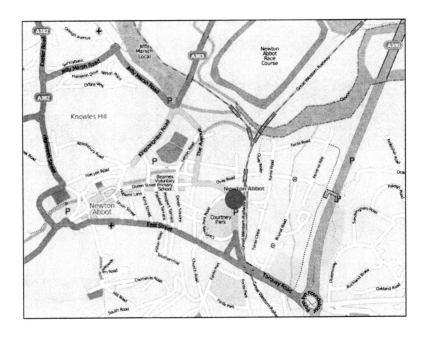

After entering Halcyon Road near the ASDA superstore, continue for 0.5 of a mile to the first roundabout. Turn right into The Avenue and continue for a further 0.3 of a mile to a set of traffic lights. Bear left into Queen Street and continue for 0.2 of a mile. Newton Abbot Railway Station is located on the left. Visitors can park for free in the short-stay car park (twenty minutes), which is situated directly opposite the doors to the main station building.

# Notes on Location 13

Newton Abbot Railway Station (originally 'Newton') was opened on Wednesday 30 December 1846 by South Devon Railway Company. On 1 February 1876, the Mortenhampstead and South Devon Railway (amalgamated 1872) was subsumed by the Great Western Railway. The original station comprised of two (later three) small train sheds each covering a separate platform for trains running to Plymouth, Exeter and Torquay. During 1861, the station was rebuilt and a single large train shed spanned all three platforms. The present station building is called South Devon House and it was opened by Lord Mildmay of Flete on 11 April 1927 (see Plate 61). It is operated by First Great Western.

Newton Abbot Railway Station is notable for three reasons. Firstly, it is feasible that ACD began a journey to Sherborne from there on Monday 3 June 1901 having spent the previous night with BFR at Park Hill House (see page 89). Secondly, it is likely that ACD met Jean Leckie at this station on Saturday 23 August 1902 with the intention of showing her some of the 'Baskerville Moor Country' (see page 15). Finally, BFR's body was taken to Newton Abbot Railway Station from London Paddington Station on Thursday 24 January 1907, prior to his funeral at St. Andrew's Church in Ipplepen. The hearse was followed by a cortege that comprised of one 'Brougham carriage', several 'buses' and five 'Landau carriages'. One of the buses was filled with floral tributes and it had to make a return journey to the railway station to collect more. These floral tributes included one with a card that read 'In loving memory of an old and valued friend from Arthur Conan Doyle.'

# Location 14
# (52.9 miles)

# Recreation Ground

### Coach Road
### Wolborough
### Newton Abbot
### TQ12 1EJ

### Latitude: 50.522493
### Longitude: -3.606509

Plate 62. The cricket pavilion at Newton College (1903). The
main 'School House' building is visible
in the background (right).

# Directions to
# Location 14

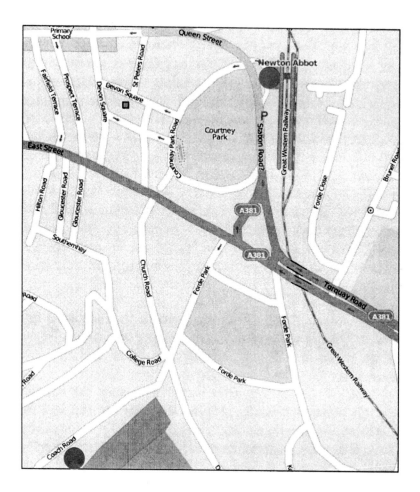

From Newton Abbot Railway Station, turn left into Station
Road. After 0.2 of a mile, turn right towards Totnes (A3081).
Continue for 100 yards and then turn left into Forde Park.
Continue for a further 100 yards and then bear right onto Coach
Road. After 0.2 of a mile, turn left into the car park of 'Devon
County Football Association Headquarters'. Visitors can park
for free directly opposite the Recreation Ground.

# Notes on Location 14

BFR was enrolled as a day boy at 'Newton College' between April 1882 and April 1890. The school campus comprised of a recreation ground, a cricket pavilion (see Plate 62), a gymnasium, multiple racquet and fives courts, a bathing pond, a chapel, reading and sitting rooms, a library, a laboratory, classrooms and two sizable boarding houses called School-House and Red House. Adjacent to the senior campus was a third junior boarding house called Newton Hall. Other notable Old-Newtonians include the author, Sir Arthur Quiller-Couch (1863-1944) and the South American explorer, Colonel Percy Harrison Fawcett (1867-1925). It is notable that Quiller-Couch met ACD on 6 March 1892. Moreover, Fawcett provided assistance to ACD with the setting for his story, *The Lost World* (1912).

Newton College shut in 1939 and most of the remaining boys and staff were transferred to Newton House at Kelly College in Tavistock (1940). The former Newton College campus was reopened as the Forde Park Home Office Approved School (1940-1973). Devon County Council then used the site as a home for vulnerable young people. Recently the site was sold to 'Barratt Developments PLC' and the buildings demolished and replaced with modern homes. However, the former Newton College recreational ground still exists and is used jointly by Devon County Council, Devon County Football Association and Newton Abbot Athletic Football Club. The latter organisation incorporated the original pavilion into its new clubhouse. The bathing-pool was filled in and is now the site of Decoy BMX track.

# Location 15
# (55.9 miles)

## *Park Hill House

**Park Hill Cross**
**Ipplepen**
**Newton Abbot**
**TQ12 5TN**

**Latitude: 50.491620**
**Longitude: -3.629034**

Plate 63. Park Hill House was the former residence of BFR. He also owned the property between July 1906 and January 1907.

# Directions to
# Location 15

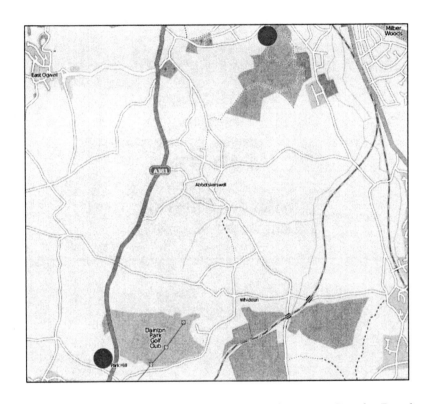

From the Recreation Ground, turn left onto Coach Road. Continue for 0.4 of a mile past St. Mary the Virgin Church to a large roundabout. Take the first exit towards Totnes (A381) and then continue for 2.1 miles to Park Hill Cross Service Station. Visitors wishing to use the facilities offered at this service station can park for free upon the forecourt. Park Hill House (see Plate 63) is situated directly opposite Park Hill Cross Service Station. This property is best viewed from atop the grassy bank, beside the footpath, that runs alongside this service station.

# Notes on Location 15

Park Hill House was constructed in around 1850 for a cider merchant called John Bowden. This estate also included a nearby farm, outbuildings and many acres of land. During 1866, John Bowden financed the construction of Ipplepen Methodist Chapel. By 1878, he was trading as a 'Corn Factor, Commission and General Merchant' in Plymouth and the neighbouring Parish of Wolborough-with-Newton Abbot. By 3 April 1881, the Bowden family had relocated to 22 Lambourn Road, Clapham, London (SW4) and Park Hill House was left unoccupied. Meanwhile, Joseph Fletcher Robinson and his second wife, Emily Robinson (née Hobson), were residing at 6, Lyndhurst Road, Wavertree near Liverpool. Ten year old BFR was boarding at a small school called Penkett Road Beach House in Liscard near New Brighton in West Cheshire.

By 3 April 1881, Joseph had retired as the commercial manager of Meade-King, Robinson & Company Limited, a firm of merchants that he had founded in around 1866 (the company still trades). In around Easter 1882, Joseph and his family relocated to Park Hill House that is situated some two-hundred and seventy miles to the south of Liverpool. One possible reason for this move is that Joseph wished to retire to an area that would enable him to pursue his interest in equestrian sports. Indeed, it is feasible that he visited Devon between 1848 and 1866, whilst working as a commercial traveller for Robert Sumner & Company of Liverpool. Furthermore, he may have visited Park Hill House itself, in order to continue trading with John Bowden because a 'Cider Merchant' of that same name is listed in *Gore's Directory for Liverpool* until 1849. Later, a 'Bowden' acted as a Witness to the marriage between BFR and Gladys Morris in London on 3 June 1902.

In the letter that ACD sent to his mother from the Duchy Hotel, he reported that 'Tomorrow we drive 16 miles to Ipplepen where R's parents live.' Other comments made within that same letter reveal that this trip was scheduled to take place on Sunday 2 June 1901. It is not known for sure whether BFR and ACD actually visited Park Hill House together but in any event, the coach house used to garage the vehicle in which they travelled is now called Park Hill Lodge and it is situated two doors to the left of Park Hill House alongside Moor Road (see Plate 64).

Plate 64. Park Hill Lodge housed the carriage that was used by Henry Baskerville to drive BFR and ACD across Dartmoor.

# Location 16
# (56.5 miles)

## *Honeysuckle Cottage

**2 Wesley Terrace
East Street
Ipplepen
Newton Abbot
TQ12 5SX**

**Latitude: 50.489354
Longitude: -3.638835**

Plate 65. 2 Wesley Terrace (right) was the home of
Henry 'Harry' Baskerville at the time that he drove
BFR and ACD across Dartmoor (1901).

# Directions to
# Location 16

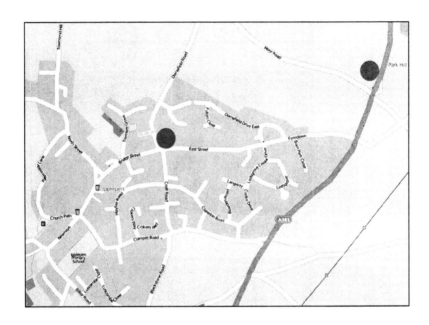

From Park Hill Cross Service Station, turn left onto the A381 towards Totnes. Continue for 100 yards and then turn right into Foredown Road (sign posted 'Ipplepen', 'Torbryan' and 'B'hempston'). Continue for 0.4 of a mile to a staggered crossroads where East Street merges with Bridge Street (just beyond the entrance to Ipplepen Methodist Chapel). At this crossroads, turn right into Dornafield Road and continue for 50 yards. Visitors can park for free on the left, just beyond the entrance to Brook Road. Walk 50 yards to the entrance of the chapel, then a further 20 yards along East Street to 2 Wesley Terrace or 'Honeysuckle Cottage' (see Plate 65). Visitors may also wish to view a nearby bench and plaque that are dedicated to the memory of BFR (see Plate 66 and Plate 67). These memorials are situated just beyond the bus stop on Bridge Street (200 yards from the staggered crossroads).

# Notes on Location 16

Henry Matthews Baskerville was born in the neighbouring village of Dainton during February 1871. His father, John Baskerville, was a farm labourer and had married Mary Matthews on 17 March 1854. The Baskervilles already had two children called John (also a farm labourer) and Mary Catherine (aged 11 and 8 years respectively).

In around 1886, Joseph Fletcher Robinson employed Henry as a 'Domestic' at Park Hill House. Initially, his duties consisted of pumping water to the house from a nearby well, polishing silverware and cleaning out fireplaces. By 1891, he had assumed the additional duties of 'Coachman and Groom' and was paid 12 shillings and 6 pence per week. Later, Henry became the head coachman and he was responsible for one assistant coachman, three coaches and two horses. He worked for the Robinson family for about twenty years until 1905.

In 1891, Henry was residing with his parents and his uncle and namesake, Henry Matthews (a retired Coachman) at what is now 2 Wesley Terrace. On 17 November 1894, Henry married Alice Perring at the Wesley Church in Torquay and thereafter the couple resided at number 3 Wesley Terrace (or 'Wisteria Cottage'). Henry and Alice had two daughters called Myrtle Alberta (born autumn 1895) and Eunice Freda (born summer 1902). By 31 March 1901, Baskerville's parents had relocated to nearby 'Credefords'.

Plate 66. The 'BFR Memorial Bench and Plaque' at Bridge Street in Ipplepen. Both items were donated to Ipplepen Parish Council by the present authors in 2009.
THE BRIAN PUGH COLLECTION.

Bertram Fletcher Robinson
1870 - 1907
Journalist, Editor, Author and
former resident of Ipplepen
He is best remembered
for assisting
Arthur Conan Doyle with
'The Hound of the Baskervilles'

Plate 67. The inscription on the 'BFR Memorial Plaque'.
THE BRIAN PUGH COLLECTION.

160

# Location 17
# (56.9 miles)

# St. Andrew's Church

### Ipplepen
### Newton Abbot
### TQ12 5RZ

## Latitude:  50.487344
## Longitude:  -3.645420

Plate 68.  BFR's grave in the north-western
section of St. Andrew's Church.
THE BRIAN PUGH COLLECTION.

# Directions to
# Location 17

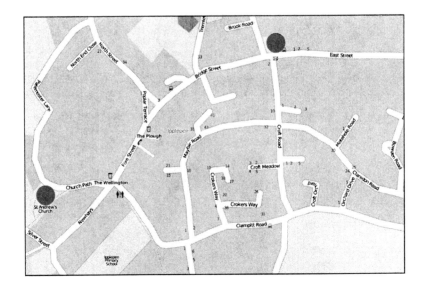

From Dornafield Road, double back to the staggered crossroads beside the chapel and turn right into Bridge Street. Continue for 0.4 of a mile towards Ipplepen Village Hall and then bear right into Silver Street. After 50 yards, park for free on the left, opposite the sign for 'Orley Road'. Cross the road and enter St. Andrew's Church through the main gate.

# Notes on Location 17

To locate BFR's grave from the main gate (see Plate 68) turn left before the first grave that belongs to the parents of Henry Baskerville (see Plate 69). Continue for 50 yards past the north-western corner of the church and towards the Church Hall. Turn left just beyond the grave of Arthur William Poole and just before the iron-gate at the entrance to the Church Hall. Continue for another 20 yards towards the first and largest monument bearing a cross. BFR is buried next to his parents and just 20 yards to the north of the Revd Robert Duins Cooke, who assisted him with mapping-out the provisional fictional setting for *The Hound of the Baskervilles* during May 1901 (see Plate 70).

Visitors are encouraged to visit the Chancel inside the church where they will locate two stained-glass windows that are dedicated to the Robinson family. The Victorian artist C.E. Kemp, who also produced windows for Yorkminster Cathedral, designed both of these windows. The southern window was commissioned by Emily Robinson to commemorate her husband, Joseph Fletcher Robinson (d. 11 August 1903). Joseph had contributed to the restoration of St. Andrew's Church and also acted as churchwarden for twenty-one years. This window bears an inscription and it depicts the figures of Our Lady and Child with St. John the Divine and St. Andrew (see Plate 71). The northern window was commissioned by BFR to commemorate his mother, Emily Robinson (d. 14 July 1906). This window depicts the Good Shepherd with St. Peter and St. Paul. BFR died just six months after his mother and his name was added to the inscription on Emily's window (see Plate 72).

Plate 69. The grave of Henry Baskerville's
parents, John and Mary.

Plate 70. The grave of BFR's friend,
the Revd Robert Duins Cooke.

Plate 71. The inscription on the window that is dedicated to the memory of BFR's father, Joseph Fletcher Robinson.

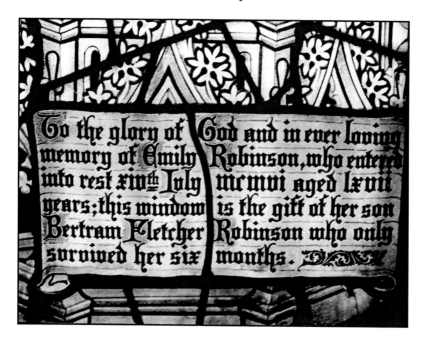

Plate 72. The inscription on the window that is dedicated to the memory of BFR's mother, Emily Robinson.

# Section 4
# Paignton & Torquay

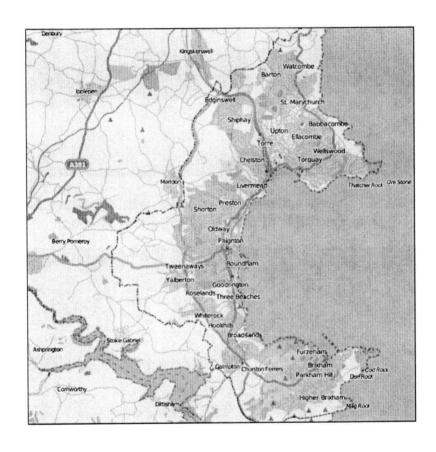

# Distance: 5.5 Miles
# Locations: 5
# Points of Interest: 5
# Driving Time: 20 Minutes
# Walking Time: 35 Minutes
# Duration: 2½ Hours

# Location 18
# (62.9 miles)

## *The Kraal

**5 Headland Grove
Paignton
TQ3 5EW**

**Latitude:  50.447532
Longitude:  -3.559625**

Plate 73.  'The Kraal' was the former home of
Henry  Paul Rabbich.  ACD stayed at
this house in August 1920.

# Directions to
# Location 18

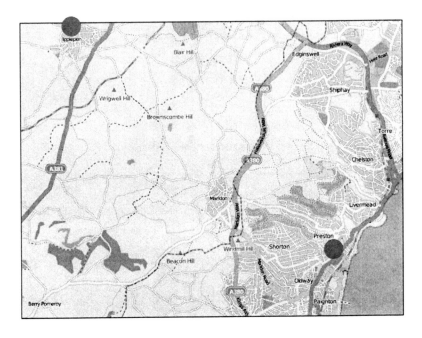

From St. Andrew's Church, double back to the T-junction between Foredown Road and the A381. Turn left and continue for 100 yards to the crossroads by Park Hill Service Station. Turn right towards Bulleigh, Compton and Marldon. Continue for 3.1 miles to a mini-roundabout situated at the exit to Marldon. At this mini-roundabout, take the first exit and continue for 100 yards. At the next roundabout, take the second exit for Preston.

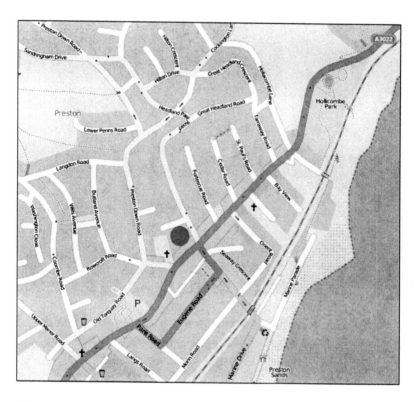

After exiting the roundabout for Preston, continue for 1.7 miles along Preston Down Road, Sandringham Gardens, Upper Headland Park Road and Headland Park Road. Shortly before reaching the traffic lights at the junction between Headland Park Road and Torquay Road (A3022), turn right into Headland Grove. 'The Kraal' is the third house on the left (see Plate 73).

# Notes on Location 18

Plate 74. Freemasons at the construction of the Masonic Lodge Hall in Courtland Road, Paignton. Henry Paul Rabbich is stood first left in the front row (1891).
PHOTOGRAPH BY KIND PERMISSION OF TORBAY LODGE No. 1358.

On 5 August 1920, ACD delivered a lecture entitled *Death and the Hereafter* to an audience at Torquay Town Hall. This meeting was presided over by Henry Paul Rabbich, the then Vice-President of the Southern Counties Union of Spiritualists. H.P. Rabbich was born during 1861 at Chudleigh in Devon and he was the son of a baker called George. By 1881, he had relocated to Paignton where he was working as a carpenter. Later, Rabbich became a prominent local builder. Amongst the many buildings that he constructed were Torbay Freemason Lodge No. 1358 (see Plate 74) and Paignton Spiritualist Church. Between 1896 and 1897, Rabbich was the Worshipful Master of that same Lodge (see Plate 75). Between 1912 and 1922, he also served as the President of Paignton Spiritualist Society.

During his 1920 trip to Torquay, ACD stayed at Rabbich's home, 'The Kraal'. This unusual name derives from a South African English word that describes an enclosure within a homestead that is surrounded by a palisade or mud wall. Rabbich lived in at least four houses that were so named during his residency in Paignton. ACD stayed in the fourth of these homes. A report from the *Paignton Observer* newspaper reveals that this house was built and occupied by Rabbich in around December 1908. By 1930, the ownership of the property had passed to his son, Percy Paul Rabbich. Percy renamed the house 'Blantyre' but the original name was subsequently restored. 'The Kraal' is still occupied by the direct descendents of H.P. Rabbich.

Plate 75. Henry Paul Rabbich during his tenure as the Worshipful Master of Torbay Masonic Lodge (1896/97).
PHOTOGRAPH BY KIND PERMISSION OF TORBAY LODGE No. 1358.

# Location 19
# (64.2 miles)

# The Grand Hotel

**Sea Front
Torquay
TQ2 6NT**

**Latitude: 50.460175
Longitude: -3.542289**

Plate 76. The southern façade of
The Grand Hotel (circa 1910).
THE BRIAN PUGH COLLECTION.

# Directions to
# Location 19

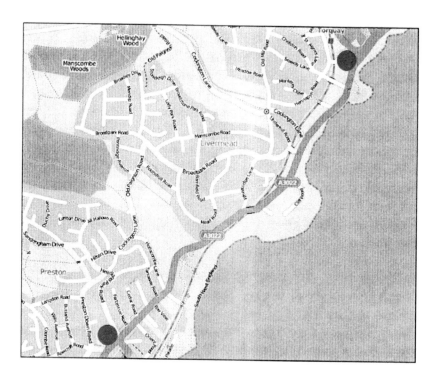

Upon exiting Headland Grove turn right and proceed to the junction between Headland Park Road and Torquay Road (A3022). At the traffic lights, turn left onto Torquay Road (which merges into Torbay Road) and continue for 1.2 miles to another set of traffic lights with signs for the Riviera International Centre, Torre Abbey and Newton Abbot. Turn left into Rathmore Road and continue for 30 yards. Turn left and either park for free on the road behind The Grand Hotel (see Plate 76) or use the pay-and-display car park at Torquay Railway Station (opposite). Non-resident visitors wishing to take refreshments at the hotel are also permitted to use their car parking facilities for free.

# Notes on Location 19

The original Torquay Railway Station (now called 'Torre Railway Station') was opened on 18 December 1848 by South Devon Railway and it enabled large numbers of wealthy Londoners to travel to Torquay in just six hours by train. On 2 August 1859, the present Torquay Railway Station was opened by Dartmoor and Torbay Railway to accommodate the ever-rising number of tourists. During the 1860s, several large hotels were constructed including the Belgrave, Victoria and Great Western (later renamed The Grand Hotel). Visitors are encouraged to take refreshments at the Compass Bar and Lounge in The Grand Hotel and enjoy the fine Art Deco architecture.

In March 1915, ACD and his second wife, Jean, resided at The Grand Hotel for two weeks. During this visit, ACD delivered a lecture at The Pavilion on the seafront that was entitled *The Great Battles of the War*. Visitors may also be interested to know that Agatha Christie (née Miller) was born in Torquay on 15 September 1890 and that she was particularly fond of The Grand Hotel. The 'Queen of Crime' wrote some 80 mystery novels during her career and invented the characters of Hercule Poirot and Miss Jane Marple. On 24 December 1914, Agatha married Colonel Archibald Christie and the newly-weds spent their honeymoon at The Grand Hotel. The couple divorced on 20 April 1928 and Agatha remarried an archaeologist, Sir Max Mallowan, on 11 September 1930. Lady Mallowan (or Dame Agatha Christie) died aged 85 years on 12 January 1976 at Cholsey in Oxfordshire.

# Location 20
# (65.1 miles)

## <u>The Pavilion Shopping Centre</u>

### Vaughan Road
### Torquay
### TQ2 5EQ

### Latitude: 50.460813
### Longitude: -3.526434

Plate 77.  The southern façade
of The Pavilion (circa 1920).
THE BRIAN PUGH COLLECTION.

# Directions to
# Location 20

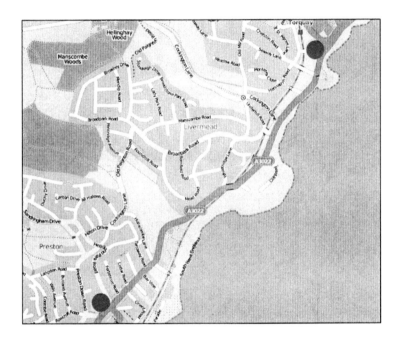

From The Grand Hotel, double back towards the traffic lights on Torbay Road opposite the seafront. Turn left and then continue for 0.8 of a mile along Torbay Road (B3199) towards the Harbour. At the first mini-roundabout take the second exit for the Marina and Pavilion. Visitors can use the Marina Car Park next to The Pavilion Shopping Centre (a small fee is charged for parking).

# Notes on Location 20

The Pavilion (see Plate 77) was opened in August 1912 as an entertainment venue. It was designed by Major Henry A. Garrett and then constructed by Robert E. Narracott. The building combines a mix of Classical and Art Nouveau styles. The façade was decorated with Doulton's Carrara enamelled stoneware to create a white palatial effect. The central copper-covered dome is topped with a full-size figure of Britannia, a symbol of patriotism and imperialism. The auditorium had oak panelling, moulded plasterwork and a curved balcony. The Pavilion building was reopened during 1987 as The Pavilion Shopping Centre.

In July 1914, ACD returned from a tour of North America. Shortly thereafter, WWI began and ACD founded a volunteer home guard unit at Crowborough and started writing regularly about the war for *The Daily Chronicle*. On 2 September 1914, ACD was invited to attend a meeting by Charles Masterman MP, who was head of the War Propaganda Bureau. ACD, H.G. Wells, G.K. Chesterton, Thomas Hardy, Rudyard Kipling and other leading British writers were recruited by Masterman to promote the British war effort through their writing. On 30 September 1914, ACD published a recruiting pamphlet for the armed forces entitled *To Arms!* During December 1914, ACD had the first of many articles about the war published by *The Strand Magazine*. This serialisation was later republished as a six-volume history entitled *The British Campaign in France and Flanders*. In February 1915, ACD commenced a tour of at least six British towns and cities to deliver a speech on *The Great Battles of the War*. The last of these talks was given at The Pavilion in Torquay on 27 March 1915. He later returned on 21 February 1923 to deliver a lecture entitled *The New Revelation*.

# Location 21
# (66.3 miles)

# *Hesketh House

**15 Hesketh Crescent**
**Torquay**
**TQ1 2LJ**

**Latitude: 50.458064**
**Longitude: -3.508582**

Plate 78.  The southern façade of Hesketh Crescent.
Hesketh Place is located to the far right (circa 1870).
THE SADRU BHANJI COLLECTION.

# Directions to
# Location 21

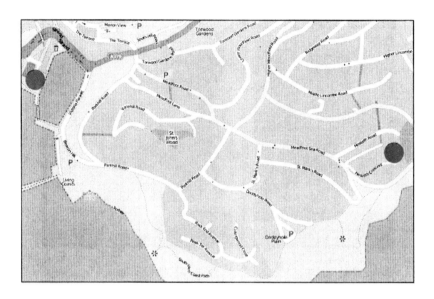

From the Marina Car Park, return to the mini-roundabout and then take the second exit for Cary Parade (B3199). Continue for 200 yards along Cary Parade and the Strand (keeping the Marina to the right). At the first roundabout take the second exit for Victoria Parade. Continue along Victoria Parade, Beacon Hill and Park Hill Road past both the Imperial Hotel and Devonshire Hotel respectively. At the junction between Park Hill Road and Meadfoot Sea Road turn right. Continue past the turning for Hesketh Road and enter Hesketh Crescent via the gateway at the entrance to the Osborne Hotel. Visitors may park for free in the spaces provided on either side of this gateway.

# Notes on Location 21

Plate 79. A wall mounted plaque at 2 Hesketh Crescent
that commemorates the building's architects.

Hesketh Crescent was commissioned during 1846 and it was
completed in 1848 (see Plate 78). It was designed by architects
John Tapley Harvey and William Harvey (see Plate 79). The
Crescent is based upon the Regency ideals of London and
Brighton, and it has attracted many notable visitors including
Charles Darwin (see Plate 80). Originally, the building had
forty-seven windows on both the first and second floors. In
addition, both of the end houses and the central house had more
ornamentation. At first named Meadfoot Crescent, it later
became Hesketh Crescent after the birth of the first son to Maria
Palk, daughter of Lord and Lady Hesketh and the wife of
Lawrence Palk. The Palks were prominent landowners and
were responsible for much of the development of Victorian
Torquay and her harbour. The Crescent is now largely occupied
by the prestigious Osborne Hotel.

During the late 1880s and the 1890s, GN had a winter residence at 'Hesketh House', 15 Hesketh Crescent. He was a keen sailor and may have been attracted to the area because of the deep water marina and harbour. Indeed, his own private yacht *The Albion* was just a few inches shorter than Queen Victoria's yacht, *HMS Britannia*. During 1887, Hesketh Crescent was put up for auction but it failed to make the reserve price. It has proved difficult to ascertain when GN acquired Hesketh House, but he may well have stepped in when the property was left unsold at auction. It was while staying at Hesketh House that GN received and dealt with a letter from William Thomas Stead containing his proposal for what was to become the *Review of Reviews* (see page 48).

Plate 80. A wall mounted plaque at 2 Hesketh Crescent that commemorates Charles Darwin's stay there.

181

# Location 22
# (68.4 miles)

## Torquay Town Hall

### Castle Circus
### Torquay
### TQ1 3DR

### Latitude:  50.468562
### Longitude:  -3.531810

Plate 81.  The southern façade of
Torquay Town Hall (circa 1900).

# Directions to
# Location 22

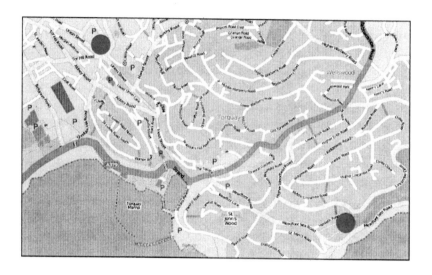

From Hesketh Crescent, double back to the roundabout near the entrance to the Marina Car Park and The Pavilion Shopping Centre. Take the second exit onto Torbay Road (B3199) and after 0.4 of a mile turn right into Belgrave Road. Continue along Belgrave Road for 300 yards (past the Victoria Hotel where ACD resided on 20 February 1923) and then take the second turning on the right (sign posted Lucius Street and Post Office). Continue along Tor Church Road and past The Majestic Templestowe Hotel (where the first Lady Conan Doyle and her mother stayed in March 1901). At the crossroads, continue along Tor Hill Road and take the first left into Morgan Avenue. Park for free in the bays located on the right. Walk to the junction of Tor Hill Road with Morgan Avenue and immediately cross the road. Walk 100 yards in the direction of the tall clock tower that forms part of Torquay Town Hall (see Plate 81). Visitors can enter the reception area and request a free tour of the building.

# Notes on Location 22

Torquay Town Hall was opened in August 1913 just twelve months after The Pavilion. The building is English renaissance in style and the clock tower above the main entrance rises to a height of two hundred feet. The building is constructed from stone and marble supplied by various local quarries including one at Ipplepen. The Grand Hall on the second floor is capable of seating twelve-hundred guests with an additional three-hundred in the gallery. It was in this room that ACD delivered a lecture entitled *Death and the Hereafter* (5 August 1920). This meeting was presided over by Henry Paul Rabbich, the then President of Paignton Spiritualist Society and Vice-President of the Southern Counties Union of Spiritualists. ACD stayed with Rabbich at his home, 'The Kraal', 5 Headland Grove, Preston, Paignton (see pages 167-171). It is not known whether the second Lady Conan Doyle accompanied ACD on this occasion.

In 1894, ACD became a life-long member of the London-based Society for Psychical Research. During November 1916, he publically declared his conversion to Spiritualism in an article entitled *A New Revelation. Spiritualism and Religion* that was published in a psychic magazine called *Light*. In 1918, ACD expanded upon his beliefs within a book entitled *The New Revelation*. Shortly thereafter, ACD's eldest son, Captain Arthur Alleyne 'Kingsley' Conan Doyle, and also his younger brother, Brigadier-General John Francis 'Innes' Hay Doyle both died from post-war influenza (Monday 28 October 1918 and Wednesday 19 February 1919 respectively). ACD was 'deeply affected' by these loses but he was comforted by his most earnest belief in Spiritualism.

# Section 5
# Exeter & Topsham

**Distance: 5.8 Miles**
**Locations: 3**
**Points of Interest: 6**
**Driving Time: 30 Minutes**
**Walking Time: 30 Minutes**
**Duration: 2 Hours**

# Location 23
# (92.6 miles)

## <u>Topsham Cemetery</u>

**Elm Grove Road**
**Topsham**
**EX3 0BW**

**Latitude: 50.689646**
**Longitude: -3.463164**

Plate 82. The Hamilton family graves in the north-western section of Topsham Cemetery. The marker for Dora Hamilton's grave is located front and centre.

# Directions to
# Location 23

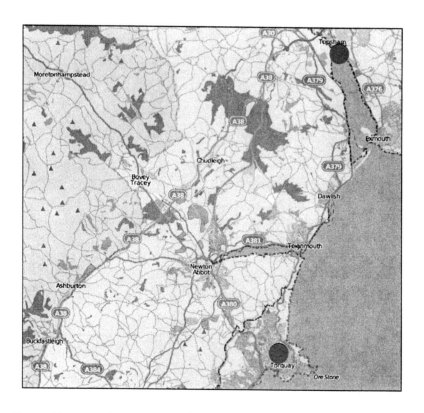

From Morgan Avenue, continue up the hill and rejoin Tor Hill Road. Follow the one-way system along Tor Hill Road and East Street. At the end of the one way system, proceed onto Newton Road (A3022). Continue along Newton Road to the traffic lights at the large crossroads between Newton Road, Hele Road and Riviera Way. Join Riviera Way (A3022) and continue to the first roundabout. At the roundabout, take the second exit onto Torquay Road (A380). Follow the road signs for Newton Abbot and Exeter to Penn Inn Roundabout. At this roundabout, take the second exit onto Besigheim Way (A380). Continue to follow signs for Exeter and join the A38 at the bottom of Telegraph Hill. Continue to the M5 Motorway and leave it at Junction 30.

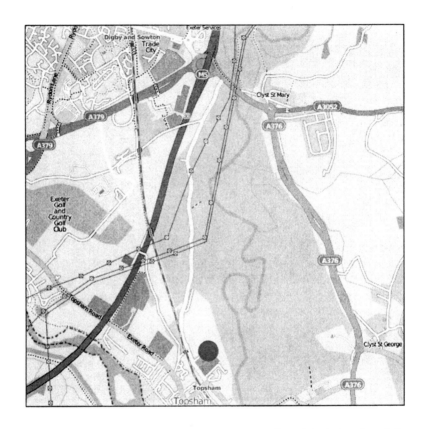

Upon exiting the M5 motorway at Junction 30, join the right-hand lane and continue to the roundabout. At the roundabout, follow signs for Exmouth and take the fourth exit onto Sidmouth Road (A376). Continue to the next roundabout and then double-back towards the M5 and Exeter. After 0.5 of a mile, turn left into Sandygate and continue along Clyst Road until it merges into Elm Grove Road. Topsham Cemetery is located on the left. Visitors can park for free along Elm Grove Road.

# Notes on Location 23

Plate 83. The marker for the grave of Dora
Geraldine Hamilton and her husband, Arthur.

On 1 February 1897, ACD travelled to Devon to meet the
family of a woman that had caught the eye of his twenty-three
year old brother 'Innes' (see pages 10-12). The girl in question
was Dora Geraldine Hamilton (1877-1950). Dora eventually
married a Royal Artillery officer called Major Arthur William
Bolton Gordon. The couple had two children, a daughter named
Phoebe Gordon (b. 1904) and a son called Kelso Gordon (b.
1909). Dora was buried in Topsham Cemetery on 12 January
1950 alongside six other members of the Hamilton family (see
Plates 82 and 83). At the time of her death she was living in
Worthing in West Sussex. Arthur was interned in the same
grave as Dora on 22 September 1952. It is possible that the
nearby Gordon Road is named after both Dora and Arthur.

Visitors may also be interested to learn that Dora's grave is located near that of Tryphena Sparks (see Plate 84). She was the first cousin and possible lover of Thomas Hardy (1840-1928) and the inspiration for his poem, *Thoughts of Phena at News of Her Death* (March 1890). On 15 December 1877, Tryphena married a local publican called Charles Frederick Gale. She died from a 'Rupture' that was caused by the birth of her fourth child. On 12 October 1892, both Thomas Hardy and ACD attended the funeral service for Lord Alfred Tennyson at Westminster Abbey. On 2 September 1914, both men were recruited by the British Liberal Party politician and journalist, Charles Masterman to work for the War Propaganda Bureau. Thomas Hardy is perhaps best remembered for his two novels, *Far from the Madding Crowd* and *Tess of the d'Urbervilles* (1874 and 1891 respectively).

Plate 84. The grave of Tryphena Sparks
(1851-1890) at Topsham Cemetery.
PHOTOGRAPH BY CHARLES POTTER ©2010.

# Location 24
# (93.6 miles)

## *The Retreat

**The Retreat Drive
Topsham
EX3 0LS**

**Latitude: 50.689437
Longitude: -3.476819**

Plate 85. The south-eastern façade of The Retreat
shortly after it was damaged by a fire (1907).
THE SADRU BHANJI COLLECTION.

# Directions to
# Location 24

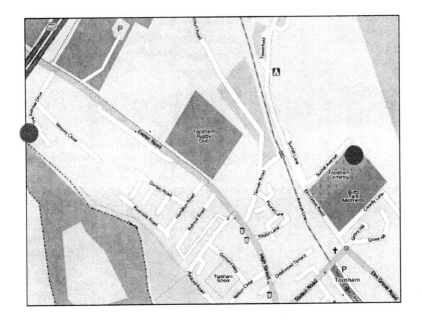

From Topsham Cemetery continue east for a further 100 yards. At the mini-roundabout, take the second exit for Station Road. Continue for 100 yards and then turn right into Fore Street which merges into both High Street and Exeter Road. Continue for 0.7 of a mile past Nelson Close, Ashford Road, Retreat Road and Hamilton Road and then turn left into The Retreat Drive. Visitors can park for free near the junction of The Retreat Drive with Wessex Close. 'The Retreat' is located a short walk away to the east of the Retreat Boatyard.

# Notes on Location 24

Plate 86. Topsham Cycling Club at 'The Retreat' (1905).
Alexander Kelso Hamilton is seated fourth from left.

ACD wrote to his mother that he intended to attend a dance at 'The Retreat' on Tuesday 2 February 1897 (see Plate 85). This house was built in around 1770 by Robert Orme on the site of a sugar refinery, but by 1781 it had passed into the hands of Alexander Hamilton (1732-1809). A self-made man, he came from a Scottish family and made his money through the East India Company and a sugar plantation in the West Indies. He served as High Sheriff for Devon and in 1786 he was part of a delegation that travelled to London to congratulate King George III upon his recent assignation escape and was knighted.

Sir Alexander Hamilton married, but he died childless. His heir was his nephew, Alexander Hamilton Kelso of Ayrshire. At Sir Alex's request he changed his name to Hamilton. The now Alexander Hamilton Hamilton died in 1853 and he was briefly

193

succeeded by his second son, Alexander Edward Hamilton. After Alexander Edward's death in 1855, his widow occupied 'The Retreat' until her son, Alexander Kelso Hamilton, came of age (see Plate 86). He became heavily involved in local affairs and was appointed High Sheriff of Devon in 1885. He was probably responsible for adding a large ball and billiard-room to 'The Retreat'. After his death, in 1929, 'The Retreat' was left to his daughter, Mrs Dora Geraldine Gordon, but it was put up for sale in 1931. The surrounding parkland was broken up into lots and by 1938 'The Retreat' was split into five flats. The walled garden and coach house later became a boatyard, and in 1969 Alexander Kelso Hamilton's ballroom was rebuilt as a private house.

Alexander Kelso Hamilton was both a keen sailor and cyclist (see Plate 86) and he named one of his boats after his daughter, 'Dora'. There is a monument to his father, Alexander Edward Hamilton within the churchyard at St. Margaret's Parish Church in Topsham. There is a second monument to Sir Alexander Hamilton in the north transept of that same church. The Hamilton family is also commemorated by way of a stained-glass window within the chapel of Topsham Cemetery.

# Location 25
# (98.4 miles)

## *Higher Barracks

**The Quadrangle**
**Horseguards**
**Exeter**
**EX4 4UX**

**Latitude: 50.731393**
**Longitude: -3.530098**

Plate 87. The eastern façade of the officer's Mess Block
and Quarters at the former Higher Barracks.

# Directions to
# Location 25

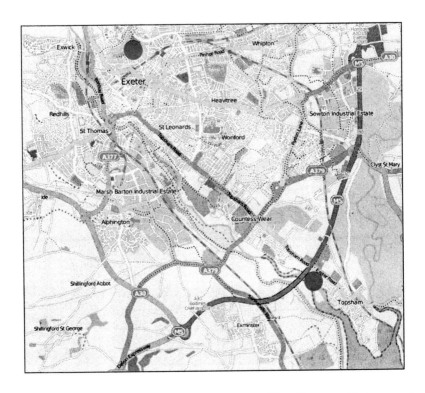

Double-back to the junction between The Retreat Drive and
Exeter Road. Turn left onto Exeter Road and drive under the
M5 Motorway. Continue along Exeter Road in the direction of
'All Routes' and 'City Centre B3182'. At the Countess Wear
Roundabout, stay in the middle lane and take the second exit for
Topsham Road. Continue along Topsham Road and Holloway
Street to the first set of traffic lights. At the lights, stay in the
second lane and continue towards the 'City Centre' along South
Street. At the first set of traffic lights, bear left onto Market
Street. Follow the signs for 'City Centre' until Market Street
merges with Mary Arches Street.

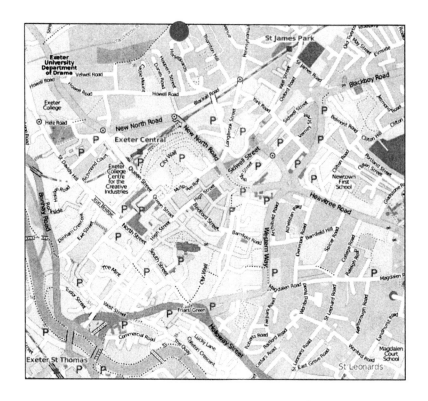

Upon entering Mary Arches Street, follow the signs for 'All Routes' and 'Guildhall'. At the traffic lights, turn right into Bartholomew Street West. Continue to the next set of traffic light and then turn left into Iron Bridge (vehicles are restricted to a width of 6 feet). Continue along Iron Bridge and St. David's Hill to a mini-roundabout. At the mini-roundabout, turn right into Hele Road and continue 100 yards to a set of traffic lights by the statue of General Sir Redvers Buller (1839-1908). At the traffic lights, turn left onto New North Road. Continue for 200 yards and then turn right onto Howell Road (just before the sign for 'The Imperial'). Continue for 0.5 of a mile (past HM Prison Exeter) and then turn left into Horseguards. Follow signs for The Quadrangle and park for free within any available unrestricted area.

# Notes on Location 25

Higher Barracks (see Plate 87) is located within the St. David's area of Exeter. It was constructed during 1794 for the cavalry in response to a perceived invasion threat from France. ACD visited Higher Barracks to see his brother 'Innes' during February 1897 and he proposed to return there with Jean Leckie in around late August 1902 (see Plate 88). Higher Barracks was originally designed to accommodate fifteen officers, one-hundred and eighty men and some two-hundred horses. The Officer's Quarters were located to the rear of the barracks and the non commissioned officers were housed in two barrack blocks on either side of it. The Officers' Quarters and one of the barrack blocks was destroyed by fire during the Nineteenth Century and each was rebuilt thereafter.

Higher Barracks was used as a military hospital in WWI. During WWII, it was used to train many a young conscript. The United States Army 500th Medical Collecting Company (60th Medical Battalion) stayed at the Higher Barracks in January 1944 during their preparations for D-Day. In 1987, the Royal Army Pay Corp was transferred to the Higher Barracks from Taunton, and they remained there until the barracks was closed during the 1990s. Higher Barracks was redeveloped into a civilian residential complex during the late 1990's by 'Barratt Developments PLC'. This same company was also responsible for redeveloping the former site of Newton Abbot Proprietary College (see Location 14).

In around the same time that Higher Barracks was built, a second such facility was constructed in Exeter. The Topsham or Artillery Barracks on Topsham Road is still in use by the military, although much of the land is now civilian residential. The officer who married Dora Hamilton, Major Arthur William Bolton was based there.

Plate 88. The north-eastern façade of the former
Higher Barrack's Guard House (off Howell Road).
ACD may have shown this building to Jean Leckie
during a visit to Exeter in around August 1902. It has
since been redeveloped into several residential properties.

# Section 6
# Lynton

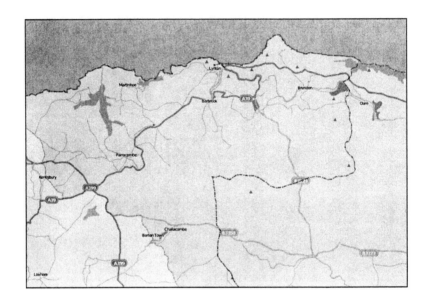

Distance: 1.0 Mile
Locations: 5
Points of Interest: 12
Driving Time: 5 Minutes
Walking Time: 45 Minutes
Duration: 2 Hours

# Location 26
# (154.6 miles)

# *The Old Station House

## Station Hill
## Lynton
## EX35 6LB

### Latitude: 51.223838
### Longitude: -3.835630

Plate 89. The eastern façade of the narrow gauge Lynton Railway Station (1906).

# Directions to
# Location 26

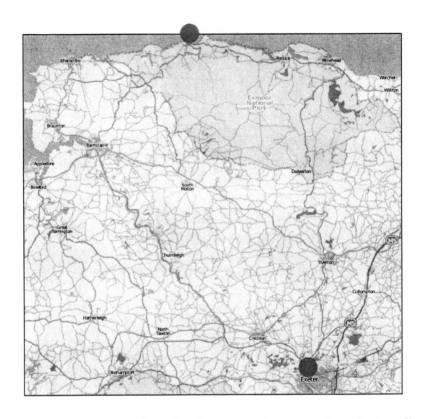

Double-back to the junction between Horseguards and Howell
Road. Turn left and continue for 50 yards to the junction
between Howell Road and Blackall Road. Turn right and
continue to the first mini-roundabout. At the mini-roundabout,
turn right onto New North Road (B3183). Continue to the end
of New North Road where it merges with Cowley Bridge Road
(A377). Continue for 0.75 of a mile to a roundabout and then
take the second exit towards Tiverton (A396). Continue for
12.5 miles to and beyond Tiverton following the signs for
'Barnstaple A361'. At the Bolham Roundabout, take the second
exit for Barnstaple (A361).

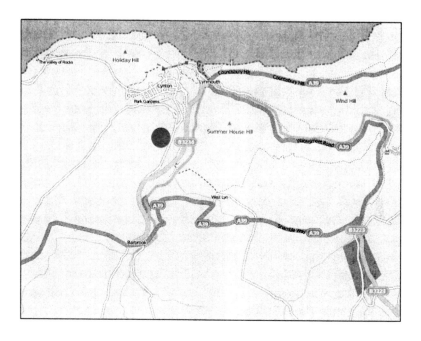

After joining the A361 for Barnstaple, continue for 19 miles to the North Aller Roundabout. At this roundabout, take the third exit for Blackmoor Gate (A399). Upon arrival at Blackmoor Gate, turn right towards Lynton and Lynmouth (A39). Continue to Barbrook and then turn left onto the Barbrook Road (B3234). Continue for 0.6 of a mile and then take the first turning on your left for Station Hill. 'The Old Station House' is located 0.3 of a mile along this road on the left-hand side. Visitors can park for free just beyond The Old Station House building.

# Notes on Location 26

The Old Station House was the terminus for the former Lynton and Barnstaple Railway (L&B). ACD was a frequent rail passenger and it is probable that he used Lynton Station (see Plate 89) for a visit to the town in September 1902. The L&B was founded shortly after 27 June 1895 and GN was the first Chairman of the Board. In September 1895, construction of Lynton Station began and Lady Newnes cut the first sod. The line was opened on 11 May 1898, and it quickly became famous for its scenic beauty and unusually narrow gauge (1ft 11½in). From 1922 the line was operated by the Southern Railway Company but the journey between Barnstaple and Lynton proved both uncomfortable and slow (1½ hours). The line was eventually closed on 29 September 1935. During 2004, a one mile section of the original line was re-opened between Woody Bay Station (three miles southwest of Lynton) and Killington Lane Halt near Parracombe.

Originally providing accommodation for the stationmaster and his family, Lynton Station was substantially updated under the ownership of Southern Railway Company. A separate house was built for the stationmaster on the rising ground to the west of the main line, and rail access to the engine shed was reversed at around the same time. The former goods shed has since been divided into two cottages and a number of private residences have been built close to the trackbed on the approaches to the former station. The station building is now a private residence but the owners have retained many of the original features including some signs (see Plate 90) and some narrow gauge track. There is also the remains of a narrow gauge locomotive situated to the rear of the building (see Plate 91).

Plate 90. An example of one of the original railway signs that has been preserved at The Old Station House at Lynton.

Plate 91. A narrow gauge locomotive that is located at the rear of The Old Station House.

# Location 27
# (155.4 miles)

## Lynton Town Hall

**Lee Road
Lynton
EX35 6BT**

**Latitude: 51.230304
Longitude: -3.836361**

Plate 92.  The north-eastern façade of Lynton Town Hall.
The building atop the hill is Hollerday House (1900).
COURTESY OF JOHN TRAVIS ©1997.

# Directions to
# Location 27

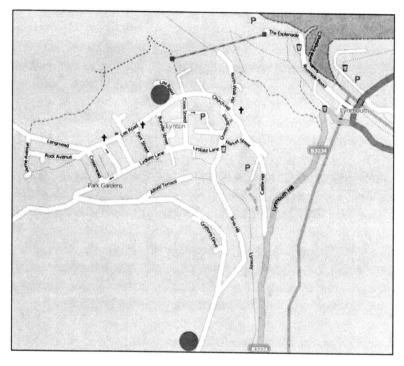

From The Old Station House, continue down Station Hill to Lydiate Lane. Follow the signs for 'Town Centre' and 'Car Park' and then take the first left onto Crossmead. Continue to the T-junction between Crossmead and Lee Road and then turn right. Continue along Lee Road for 300 yards to Lynton Town Hall. Visitors can park on Lee Road directly in front of the building. Alternatively, visitors can continue for a further 200 yards to the pay and display car park at Castle Hill.

# Notes on Location 27

On 11 May 1898, GN and Lady Newnes arrived at Lynton Station upon the first official L&B train. Following their arrival, they participated in an official ceremony to mark the opening of the L&B Railway. Thereafter they were driven to Lee Road by a horse-drawn carriage and Lady Newnes laid one of two foundation corner stones for Lynton Town Hall (see Plates 92 & 93). GN gifted the building to both Lynton and Lynmouth in honour of his son, Frank Hillyard Newnes, who had recently come of age (b. 28 September 1876).

Lynton Town Hall took two years to complete, at a personal cost to GN of some £20,000. It was officially opened by him on 15 August 1900 (see Plate 94). Alighting from his carriage, GN was presented with a silver key bearing his coat of arms. He unlocked the main door and then stepped inside. A few minutes later he appeared upon the balcony, and took the cheers of the crowd. After making a short speech he turned to the Chairman of the Council and handed him the keys to the building.

Despite concern from time to time over its state, Lynton Town Hall continues to serve both the community and visitor well. In addition to being available for various public functions it houses a permanent exhibition devoted to GN. It also houses two busts of GN: a bronze one that was recently placed in an outside niche (see Plate 95), and a marble one that was given pride of place on the main staircase (see page 62). The latter was a gift from the local people and it was unveiled at a ceremony that was held on 6 September 1902. ACD delivered the main dedication speech at that ceremony.

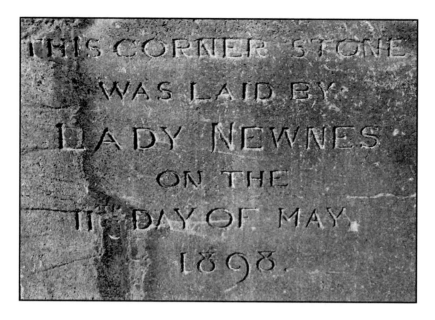

Plate 93. One of two foundation corner stones that lay either side of the main entrance to Lynton Town Hall. The second stone was laid by Ada Medland Jeune.

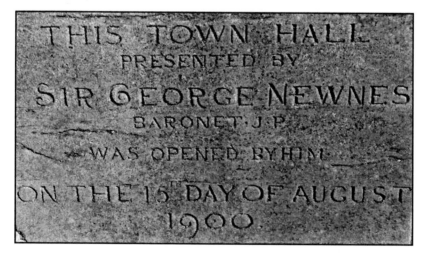

Plate 94. One of two dedication stones that lay at either side of the main entrance to Lynton Town Hall.

Plate 95. The bronze bust of Sir George Newnes that is
located in an external alcove to the left of the
main entrance at Lynton Town Hall.

# Location 28
## (155.4 miles)

## <u>Hollerday House (ruins)</u>

### Hollerday Hill
### Lynton

### Latitude: 51.234512
### Longitude: -3.840108

Plate 96. A model of the western façade of
Hollerday House as it appeared in 1900.
BY PERMISSION OF LYNTON & LYNMOUTH
TOURIST INFORMATION CENTRE.

# Directions to
# Location 28

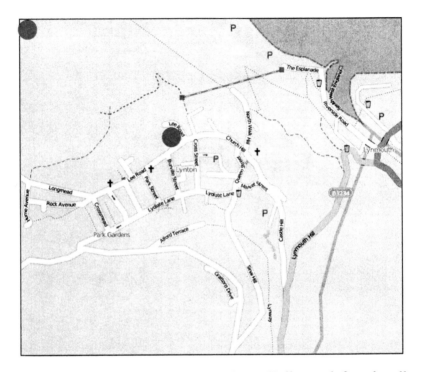

From the main entrance at Lynton Town Hall, turn left and walk past the information board. After the information board, turn left and walk alongside Lynton Town Hall towards its rear. Turn left and walk up the hill between the limestone rocks that once marked the start of the long meandering drive to Hollerday House. Continue for 100 yards along the pathway to Honey Pot Cottage. At the cottage, take the small wooded path to the right and then continue for 100 yards to the ruins of Hollerday House. Visitors will find information boards at this location with more details about both GN and Hollerday House.

# Notes on Location 28

During 1890, GN purchased Hollerday Hill with a view to building a home there. The work was supervised by a local builder called Bob Jones. The construction of the approach road began in May 1891. Eighteen months later, work began on the house itself and it was completed by the end of 1893 (see Plates 22 & 96). From then on, GN and his family spent each August, September and Christmas at their Lynton retreat. It also appears that ACD stayed at Hollerday House during his visit to Lynton in September 1902. During the summer of 1909, GN became seriously ill and he left his main residence at Putney Heath in London to recuperate in Lynton. Nevertheless, GN's health continued to wane and he died at Hollerday House on Thursday 9 June 1910.

GN left substantial debts so Frank and Lady Newnes decided to leave Hollerday House. The furniture was sold off at auction, but the house and surrounding land failed to attract any buyers. Hollerday House was shut up and left to its fate. On the night of 4 August 1913 the building caught fire and could not be saved. Although there was ample evidence of arson, the culprit has never been identified. During April 1933, the Hollerday House estate was purchased by John Holman and it was gifted by him to the people of Lynton and Lynmouth. The ruins of the house became a favourite place among the local children, but were put to more serious use during WWII as a Civil Defence training area. After the war the building was in a dangerous condition and considered to be in need of demolition. In the early 1950s, Hollerday House was duly blown up as part of a commando training exercise. Nevertheless, areas of the lawn, landscaped gardens and some dressed brickwork still remain (see Plates 97 & 98).

Plate 97. A view of the ruins of Hollerday House from the lawn area that was adjacent to the main entrance.

Plate 98. The dressed bricked work that once supported the large multi-storey bay window at the north-western corner of Hollerday House.

# Location 29
# (155.4 miles)

## <u>United Reformed Church</u>

**Lee Road**
**Lynton**
**EX35 6BS**

**Latitude: 51.229485**
**Longitude: -3.837858**

Plate 99. The western façade of
Lynton United Reformed Church.

# Directions to
# Location 29

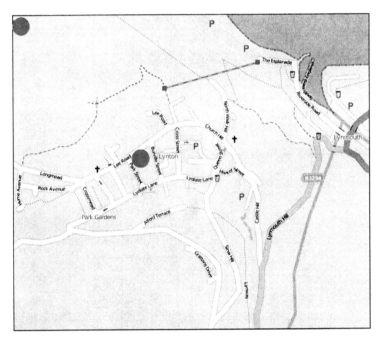

From the ruins of Hollerday House, return to Lynton Town Hall. Walk for a further 150 yards in the direction of Crossmeads. Lynton United Reformed Church (see Plate 99) is located on the left next to the junction of Lee Road with Park Street.

# Notes on Location 29

At the end of the Nineteenth Century the existing Lynton Congregational Church near the bottom of Sinai Hill was considered to be too small and inconveniently sited by many worshippers. In 1903, Bob Jones offered a plot of land in Lee Road upon which a new church could be built. Members of the congregation approached GN for some financial assistance with the project. With characteristic generosity and in memory of his father, the Revd Thomas Mold Newnes he embarked on paying some £1,500, not only for the site to be enlarged but also for a far more imposing building than was previously posited. The new Congregational (now United Reformed) Church opened for worship in August 1904. The opening services were taken by the well-known London-based preacher, the Revd Reginald John Campbell (see Plate 28). With typical liberality, GN presented him with a new motor car following the service.

During the same month as the official opening of the Lynton Congregational Church, ACD had a story entitled *The Adventure of the Missing Three-Quarter* published in *The Strand Magazine*. The story was the eleventh episode in a series of thirteen Sherlock Holmes short stories that were later compiled and republished in a book entitled *The Return of Sherlock Holmes* by George Newnes Ltd. (7 March 1905). ACD's friend, BFR contributed a central idea to the second episode in this collection of stories, *The Adventure of the Norwood Builder* (October 1903). In around August 1904, BFR commissioned the famous artist Leslie Ward ('Spy') to produce a caricature of the Revd Campbell for *Vanity Fair*. BFR edited this influential weekly journal between May 1904 and October 1906. The caricature of the Revd Campbell appeared within the issue for 24 November 1904 (see Plate 100). Leslie Ward had previously drawn GN for *Vanity Fair* (see Plate 1).

REV. R. J. CAMPBELL. 1904.

"*Fearless but intemperate.*"

Plate 100. A caricature of The Revd Campbell by Leslie Ward.
It was commissioned by BFR at around the same time
of the opening of Lynton Congregational Church.

218

# Location 30
# (155.4 miles)

# The Old Cemetery

**Longmead**
**Lynton**
**EX35 6DQ**

**Latitude: 51.229292**
**Longitude: -3.841833**

Plate 101. The grave of Sir George Newnes
at 'The Old Cemetery' in Lynton.

# Directions to
# Location 30

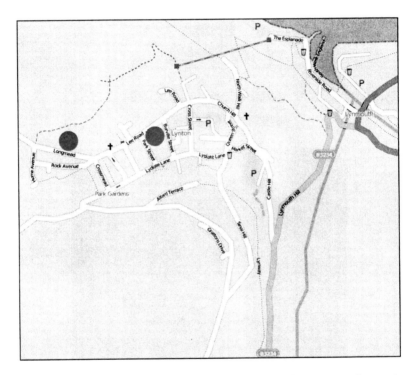

From Lynton United Reformed Church, walk 150 yards to the
junction between Lee Road and Crossmead. At this junction,
continue for a further 100 yards along Longmead. 'The Old
Cemetery' is located on the right just beyond the entrance to the
Longmead House Hotel. GN's grave (see Plate 101) is situated
within the north-western area of the graveyard opposite a small
bungelow.

# Notes on Location 30

Sir George Newnes died at Hollerday House on the morning of Thursday 9 June 1910. He was 59 years-old and had been seriously ill with diabetes for over a year. On the afternoon of Monday 13 June, his body was conveyed by local members of the Ancient Order of Foresters from Hollerday Hill to St. Mary's Church (Lee Road) and thence the cemetery. The ensuing procession included members of the Lynton Urban District Council, the Coastguard and the crew of the Lynmouth Lifeboat. The funeral service was conducted by the Revd W.E. Cox (rector), the Revd C.E. Treadwell (vicar of Lynmouth) and the Revd E.H.L. Jones (pastor of Lynton Congregational Church). The chief mourners included Frank Newnes (son), Mr and Mrs James Hillyard (brother-in-law and sister), Mr W. Newnes (brother) and Mrs Stevens (sister). A number of senior members of staff at George Newnes Limited also attended the funeral service.

Following GN's death, Frank Newnes succeeded to the title of 'Baronet of Wildcroft' and also to the Chairmanship of George Newnes Limited. On Friday 11 July 1930, he attended the funeral service for ACD at Windlesham in Crowborough. Sir Frank's mother, Lady Priscilla Newnes died some years prior to that event at Hinton Wood House in Bournemouth (see Plate 102). Lady Newnes was buried at Bournemouth Cemetery three days after her death. Frank remained the Chairman of George Newnes Limited until 1954 and thereafter he was President. He died at Perth in Western Australia on Sunday 10 July 1955 aged 78 years. Despite having married twice, Sir Frank Newnes had no children so his title became extinct upon his death.

Plate 102. The commemorative inscription that was
added to the grave of Sir George Newnes
following the death of Lady Newnes.

# Selected Bibliography

Whilst every effort has been made to follow conventions for the presentation of sources, it has not always proved possible. For example, the authors have consulted birth, marriage, death and English Census records for the four major players listed in Chapters 1-4. They have also used the last will-and-testaments of ACD, GTB, BFR, GN, Gladys Hill Robinson (BFR's wife), Sir John Richard Robinson (BFR's uncle), Henry Matthews Baskerville, Squire Richard Cabell III and others. Such records do not readily lend themselves to listing and in any case, all are available from Ancestry.com or the General Register Office. In other cases, some Nineteenth Century texts do not list the name of the author or authors and provide only partial details about the publisher. For these reasons the authors have either omitted partial entries from this Selected Bibliography or listed them with explanatory notes in square brackets. They have also elected to omit references to some on-line resources that were used in researching Chapter 5. This decision was taken in order to preserve clarity, conserve space and because many websites are transient in nature.

Andrews, C., 'The Bound of the Astorbilts' in *The Bookman*, Vol. 15, No. 4, June 1902, (New York: Dodd, Mead & Co.).

Anon., 'A Devon Coachman Whose Name Has Become Immortal', *The Western Times and Gazette*, 1 Nov 1957 [article about Henry Baskerville].

Anon., 'A Runaway Train', *Manchester Times*, 27 Aug 1881 [report on the incident that is said by some to have inspired GN to found *Tit-Bits*].

Anon., 'Ashburton Funeral – The Late Mrs. A. Baskerville', *Mid-Devon Advertiser*, 2 June 1951 [report about the funeral of Alice Baskerville, the wife of Henry Baskerville].

Anon., 'Bank-holiday in the West', *The Western Morning News*, 28 May 1901.

Anon., 'Baskerville is Dead – Conan Doyle Used His Name for Sherlock Holmes Story', *The New York Times*, USA, 2 April 1962.

Anon., 'Beyond the Veil – Sir Arthur Conan Doyle on Modern Miracles', *The Western Morning News*, 5 Aug 1920 [report on ACD's lecture at Exeter Hippodrome].

Anon., 'B.F.R.', *Daily Express*, 22 Jan 1907 [obituary].

Anon., 'Coachman was in at Birth of Baskerville Tale', *Western Evening Herald*, 29 March 1962 [Henry Baskerville obituary].

Anon., 'Congo Wrongs – Sir A. Conan Doyle and Mr. Morel at Plymouth', *The Western Morning News*, 19 Nov 1909 [article about ACD's first lecture at Plymouth Guildhall].

Anon., 'Council of Legal Education', *The Times*, 15 April 1896 [an article reporting that BFR had passed the examination for the Bar at the Inner Temple].

Anon., 'Court Circular', *The Times*, 25 Oct 1902 [item reporting that ACD had been knighted by King Edward].

Anon., 'Dartmoor in Story', *The Western Morning News*, 2 March 1931.

Anon., 'Death and the Hereafter – Sir Arthur Conan Doyle Lectures at Torquay', *The Torquay Directory and South Devon Journal*, 11 Aug 1920 [article about ACD's lecture at Torquay Town Hall].

Anon., 'Death of Mr. B. F. Robinson', *Mid-Devon and Newton Times*, 26 Jan 1907.

Anon., 'Death of Mr. B. F. Robinson', *Vanity Fair*, Jan 1907.

Anon., 'Devon Mansion Destroyed by Fire: Supposed Suffragist Outrage', *The Times*, 10 June 1910 [report on the burning down of *Hollerday House*].

Anon., 'Doctor Who Helped to Cure the City', *Bristol Evening Post*, 11 April 2006 [article about Dr William Budd, the father of GTB].

Anon., 'Do Fairies Exist? – Sir A. Conan Doyle's Belief – Manifestations in Devon & Cornwall', *The Western Morning News and Mercury*, 24 Feb 1923.

Anon., *Edinburgh Wanderers Football Club Centenary 1868 – 1968*, (Self-published: 1968).

Anon., 'Fashionable Wedding at Topsham', *Exeter Flying Post*, 19 Feb 1898 [report about the marriage between Dora Geraldine Hamilton and Major Arthur William B. Gordon].

Anon., 'Festival Sports at Forde Park School', *Mid-Devon Advertiser*, 14 June 1951.

Anon., 'Football. Blackheath v. West Kent', *The Times*, 29 Sep 1879.

Anon., 'Football. Glasgow Academicals v. Blackheath', *The Times*, 7 March 1878.

Anon., 'Football. Rugby Union Rules. London, Western, and Midland Counties v. Oxford and Cambridge', *The Times*, 10 Nov 1892.

Anon., 'Football. Rugby Union Rules. London, Western, and Midland Counties v. Oxford and Cambridge', *The Times*, 9 Nov 1893.

Anon., 'Football. Rugby Union Rules. Oxford v. Cambridge', *The Times*, 17 Dec 1891.

Anon., 'Football. Rugby Union Rules. Oxford v. Cambridge', *The Times*, 15 Dec 1892.

Anon., 'Football. Rugby Union Rules. Oxford v. Cambridge', *The Times*, 14 Dec 1893.

Anon., 'Golden Wedding Celebration – Ashburton Couple', *Western Evening Herald*, 21 Nov 1944 [article about Henry and Alice Baskerville].

Anon., 'Greatest Delusion or Greatest Fact? – Spiritualists' Claim – Sir A. Conan Doyle at Plymouth', *The Western Morning News and Mercury*, 24 Feb 1923 [article about ACD's second and final lecture at Plymouth Guildhall].

Anon., 'Henley Royal Regatta', *The Times*, 6 July 1892.

Anon., 'Henley Royal Regatta', *The Times*, 7 July 1892.

Anon., 'Henley Royal Regatta', *The Times*, 8 July 1892.

Anon., *Hesketh Crescent*, (Unpublished: n.d.), [Torquay Library: reference 'pamphlet 0981'].

Anon., 'His Name has Gone Down in Mystery – Harry Baskerville', *South Devon Journal*, 17 Oct 1951.

Anon., 'Hound of the Baskervilles – Harry Baskerville Dead; Conan Doyle Used Name', *New York Herald Tribune*, USA, 2 April 1962.

Anon., 'In Memoriam', *The World*, 22 Jan 1907 [BFR obituary].

Anon., *Ipplepen Cricket Club 1890 – 1990*, (Self-published: 1990).

Anon., 'Lady Newnes', *The Times*, 9 Oct 1939 [announcement of the death of Lady Emmeline Newnes; first wife of Sir Frank Newnes].

Anon., 'Late Mr. B. Fletcher Robinson – Funeral at Ipplepen', *The Western Morning News*, 25 Jan 1907.

Anon., 'Life After Death – Sir A. Conan Doyle on Danger of Self-Satisfied', *The Western Morning News*, 6 Aug 1920 [article about ACD's lecture at Torquay Town Hall].

Anon., 'Linked to the Hound of the Baskervilles', *Dawlish Post*, 15 Nov 1991 [article about Park Hill House].

Anon., 'London Editor's Death – Mr. B. Fletcher Robinson Succumbs to Typhoid Fever', *The Western Guardian*, 24 Jan 1907.

Anon., 'Lord Roberts and The Pilgrims', *The Times*, 20 June 1904.

Anon., *Lynton & Lynmouth Cliff Railway: Photographs and History*, (Brixham: Hamilton-Fisher & Co., n.d.).

Anon., 'Marriages – Robinson:Morris', *The Times*, 5 June 1902.

Anon., 'Mr. Baskerville Returned to see Old Village Friends', *The South Devon Journal*, 13 June 1951.

Anon., 'Mr. Fletcher Robinson – Memorial Service at St. Clement Danes', *Daily Express*, 27 Jan 1907.

Anon., 'Mystery of the Stonehouse Wall Plaque', *Waterfront News*, Winter 1994.

Anon., 'Obituary – Mr. B. Fletcher Robinson', *The Times*, 22 Jan 1907.

Anon., 'Obituary – Mr. Phil Morris, A.R.A.', *The Times*, 24 April 1902.

Anon., 'Obituary – Sir John R. Robinson', *The Times*, 2 Dec 1903.

Anon., 'Presentation at Dartmoor Prison', *The Western Morning News*, 31 May 1901.

Anon., 'Rowing. The University Boat Race', *The Times*, 12 Feb 1894 [article reporting that BFR was selected to row for the Cambridge 'Trial VIII' ahead of the annual 'Varsity Boat Race].

Anon., 'Sidelights on Great Crime Stories (No 10) – Ghost Hound of the Marshes – Was it the Inspiration of Conan Doyle's Story?' *The Evening News*, 25 May 1939.

Anon., 'Sir A. Conan Doyle – Special Interview at Torquay – Spiritualists View of Religion', *The Western Morning News and Mercury*, 21 Feb 1923.

Anon., 'Sir Arthur Conan Doyle at Torquay', *The Western Morning News*, 29 March 1915 [report on ACD's first lecture at The Pavilion in Torquay].

Anon., 'Sir Arthur Conan Doyle at Torquay', *Torquay Times*, 2 April 1915.

Anon., 'Sir Arthur Conan Doyle, Forthcoming Visit to Torquay', *Torquay Times*, 28 July 1920.

Anon., 'Sir Frank Newnes', *The Times*, 11 July 1955 [obituary].

Anon., 'Sir George Newnes', *The Times*, 10 June 1910 [obituary].

Anon., 'Some Gossip of the Week', *The Sphere*, 26 Jan 1907 [BFR obituary].

Anon., 'Spiritualism – New Town Hall, Torquay', *The Torquay Directory and South Devon Journal*, 21 July 1920 [advertising ACD's forthcoming lecture].

Anon., *The British Medical Journal*, 16 March 1889 [GTB obituary].

Anon., 'The Coronation Honours', *The Times*, 26 June 1902 [article reporting that King Edward VII had knighted ACD].

Anon., 'The Escape of Convicts', *The Times*, 17 June 1901.

Anon., 'The Life Hereafter, Sir Arthur Conan Doyle's Experience', *Paignton Observer*, 12 Aug 1920.

Anon., 'The Lynton and Barnstaple Railway', *The Times*, 28 April 1898 [report on the rail link prior to its official opening].

Anon., *The New Forest Church of All Saints Minstead*, (Minstead Parish Church Council, 1999).

Anon., 'The New Lynton and Barnstaple Railway', *The Times*, 18 Sep 1895 [a report about the ceremony to mark the start of work upon the trackbed].

Anon., 'The New Revelation – Sir A. Conan Doyle's Lecture at Torquay', *The Western Morning News and Mercury*, 22 Feb 1923 [report on ACD's second and final lecture at The Pavilion in Torquay].

Anon., 'The New Revelation – Sir Arthur Conan Doyle at Torquay – Life After Death', *Torquay Times*, 23 Feb 1923.

Anon., 'The New Revelation – Visit of Sir Arthur Conan Doyle to Torquay', *The Torquay Directory and South Devon Journal*, 28 Feb 1923.

Anon., 'The New Sherlock Holmes Story' in *The Bookman*, Oct 1901, (New York: Dodd, Mead & Co.).

Anon., 'The Original Baskerville Dies, Aged 91', *The Western Morning News*, 30 March 1962.

Anon., 'Tribute to Sir G. Newnes', *The Times*, 9 Sep 1902 [report about the unveiling of a GN bust at Lynton Town Hall].

Anon., 'University Intelligence', *The Times*, 26 Nov 1897 [item reporting that BFR was awarded an MA degree by his Alma Mater; Jesus College, Cambridge].

Anon., 'When Conan Doyle Practised Medicine in Plymouth', *The Western Morning News*, 2 Feb 1949 [brief article on ACD's links with Devon].

Anon., 'Where Sir Arthur Played Billiards', *Dawlish Post*, n.d. [article about Park Hill House].

*Aubrey and Co.'s Devon and Cornwall Directory*, 1910 (Walsall: Aubrey & Co.) [Henry Paul Rabbich is recorded as being a 'Builder' based at Victoria House, Paignton].

Austin, B., 'Dartmoor Revisited or Discoveries in Dartmoor', *Austin's Sherlockian Studies – The Collected Annuals*, (New York: Magico Magazine, 1986) [article about Richard Cabell III and the 'Baskerville Legend'].

Bainbridge, J., *Newton Abbot: A History and Celebration of the Town*, (Teffont, Salisbury: Frith, 2004).

Bamberg, R. W., *Haunted Dartmoor – A Ghost-Hunter's Guide*, (Newton Abbot: Peninsula Press, 1993).

Barber, C., *Princetown of Yesteryear* – 2 vols., (Exeter: Obelisk, 1995).

Barber, S. & Barber, C., *Dark and Dastardly Dartmoor*, (Exeter: Obelisk, 1988).

Baring-Gould, S., *A Book of Dartmoor*, (London: Methuen, 1900).

Baring-Gould, S., 'First Report of the Dartmoor Exploration Committee: The Exploration of Grimspound', *Report and Transactions of the Devonshire Association for the Advancement of Science*, Vol. 26, 1894, (Devon: The Devonshire Association).

Baskerville, H. M., 'A letter to the Editor [Noel Vinson]', *The Western Morning News*, 16 Feb 1949 [letter that is dated 9 Feb 1949 and which refers to the trip that Henry Baskerville made to Dartmoor with BFR and ACD during 1901].

Bath, E. J., *Newton Abbot Roundabout*, (Self-published, 1984) [Newton Abbot Library].

Bhanji, S., *Postcards From Topsham: Volume One*, (Exeter: Precious Moments [Exeter] Limited, 2009).

Bhanji, S., *Postcards From Topsham: Volume Two*, (Exeter: Precious Moments [Exeter] Limited, 2009).

Bigelow, S. T., [ed. Ruber, P.], 'The Singular Case of Fletcher Robinson' in *The Baker Gasogene – a Sherlockian Quarterly*, Vol. 1, No. 2, 1961, (New York) [and republished in *The Baker Street Briefs* by Toronto Reference Library during 1993].

Blathwayt, R., 'Lions in their Dens: III. George Newnes at Putney' in *The Idler*, Vol. III, March 1893.

Bond, Pearce & Co. Solicitors, *Indenture between Benjamin Butland of Leigham Barton Eggbuckland, farmer and landlord, and George Budd of East Stonehouse, surgeon and tenant*, 16 Nov 1881 [this item is held by Plymouth & West Devon Record Office: Accession No. '917/35'].

*Bradshaw's General Railway and Steam Navigation Guide*, May & June 1901 [the most complete of the numerous monthly British railway guides and timetables for that period. Available at The National Archive in Richmond: Ref. 'Rail 903/118'].

Brandenburg, B., Doyle, A. C., Green, A. K., Poe, E. A., Robinson, B. F. & Stevenson, R. L., (ed. Patten, W.), *Great Short Stories: Volume 1 Detective Stories*, (New York: P. F. Collier & Son, 1906) [this anthology of twelve short stories includes both *The Sign of Four* and *A Scandel in Bohemia* by ACD and also *The Vanished Millionaire* by BFR].

*Bristol & Clifton Directory*, 1880 & 1886, (Bristol: J. Wright & Co.).

Brown, G. A., Prideaux, J. D. C. A. & Radcliffe, H. C., *The Lynton & Barnstaple Railway*, (Newton Abbot: David and Charles, new edition, 1971).

Budd, A. J. & others, (ed. Marshall, F.), *Football: The Rugby Union Game*, (London: Cassell & Co. Ltd., 1892).

Byng, B., *Dartmoor's Mysterious Megaliths*, (Plymouth: Baron Jay, n.d.).

Carr, J. D., *The Life of Sir Arthur Conan Doyle*, (London: John Murray, 1949).

Carter, P., *Newton Abbot*, (Exeter: The Mint Press, 2004).

*Cassell's Family Magazine*, (ed. Pemberton, M.), Dec 1896 – Nov 1897, (London: Cassell, Petter & Galpin) [these issues include three articles by BFR].

*Cassell's Magazine*, (ed. Pemberton, M.), Dec 1897 – Dec 1903, (London: Cassell & Co. Ltd.) [these issues include twenty-one articles, four short stories and two poems by BFR].

Catchpole, A. T., *The Lynton & Barnstaple Railway*, (Usk: Oakwood Press, sixth edition reprinted, 1983).

*The Chanticleer*, [ed. Foakes-Jackson, J. & others], 1890-1894, (Cambridge: J. Palmer) [Jesus College magazine that changed its name to *The Chanticlere* from Oct 1892].

Chapman, L., *The Ancient Dwellings of Grimspound and Hound Tor*, (Chudleigh: Orchard Publications, 1996).

*The Cheltonian*, June 1901 [report about a cricket match played on 7-8 June between Cheltenham College and an Incogniti team that featured ACD].

*Clifton College Register 1862-1947*, 47th Edn, (Old Cliftonian Society, 1947).

*Climatological Returns for Ashburton, Druid, Devon*, May & June 1901 [daily weather records prepared for the Royal Meteorological Society by one Fabyn Amery and held by the Met Office National Meteorological Archive, Exeter: Ref. '910070'].

*Climatological Returns for Great Yarmouth, Norfolk*, April 1901 [weather records prepared for the Royal Meteorological Society and held by the Met Office National Meteorological Archive, Exeter: Ref. '910741'].

*Climatological Returns for Princetown, Devon*, May & June 1901 [weather records prepared for the Royal Meteorological Society by staff at HM Prison Dartmoor and held by the Met Office National Meteorological Archive, Exeter: Ref. '911426'].

Cooke, H. R., 'A letter to the Editor [Noel Vinson]', *The Western Morning News*, 14 Feb 1949 [this letter is dated 7 Feb

1949 and states that BFR visited Dartmoor with the Revd R.D. Cooke prior to ACD's trip there in 1901].

Cooke, R. D., *The Churches and Parishes of Ipplepen and Torbryan*, c. 1930 [this article appears to have been published as a supplement to *Ipplepen Parish Magazine*].

Cramer, W. S., (ed. Penzler, O.), 'The Enigmatic B. Fletcher Robinson and the Writing of The Hound of the Baskervilles' in *The Armchair Detective*, Vol. 26, No. 4, Autumn 1991, (New York: The Mysterious Press).

Crossing, W., *Princetown – Its Rise and Progress*, (Brixham, Devon: Quay Publications, 1989).

Croxford, C., *Lynton & Lynmouth: A Shortish Guide*, (Launceston, Cornwall: Bossiney Books, 2008).

*Daily Express*, May 1900 – June 1904, (London: C. Arthur Pearson Ltd.) [these include one hundred and two by-lined articles, 1 poem and 1 playlet by BFR].

Dam, H. J. W., 'Arthur Conan Doyle: An Appreciation of the Author of "Sir Nigel", the Great Romance Which Begins Next Sunday', *New York Tribune Sunday Magazine*, USA, 26 Nov 1905.

*Dictionary of National Biography*, (Oxford University Press, 2004) [a more 'warts and all' portrayal of GN than that provided by Friederichs].

Djabri, S. C., *The Story of the Sepulchre – The Cabells of Buckfastleigh and the Conan Doyle Connection*, (London: Shamrock Press, 1989).

*Doidge's Western Counties Yearbook, 1879-80* (Plymouth).

Doyle, A. C., 'Dry Plates on a Wet Moor' in *The Hound*, Vol. 3, 1994, (Fareham: Sherlock Publications) [originally published in *The British Journal of Photography*, Nov 1882].

Doyle. A. C., *Memories and Adventures*, (London: Greenhill Books, 1988) [a facsimile of the first edition – London: Hodder & Stoughton, 1924].

Doyle, A. C., 'My First Experiences in Practice', *The Strand Magazine*, Vol. 66, No. 395, Nov 1923, (London: George Newnes Ltd.).

Doyle, A. C., 'The Adventure of the Norwood Builder' in *Collier's Weekly Magazine*, Oct 1903, (New York: P.F. Collier & Son).

Doyle, A. C., *The Hound of the Baskervilles*, (London: George Newnes Ltd., 1902).

Doyle, A. C., *The Lost World*, (London: Hodder & Stoughton, 1912).

Doyle, A. C., *The Stark Munro Letters*, (London: Longmans, Green & Co., 1895).

Dunnill, M., *Dr. William Budd. Bristol's Most Famous Physician*, (Bristol: Redcliffe Press, 2006).

Edwards, O. D., *The Quest for Sherlock Holmes*, (Edinburgh: Mainstream Publishing, 1983).

Elvins, J. W., *Plymouth Street Directory*, 1867 & 1873, (Plymouth).

Evans, P., 'The Mystery of Baskerville', *Daily Express*, 16 March 1959.

*Eyre Brothers' Plymouth, Devonport and Stonehouse Street Directory*, 1880-1890, (London: Eyre Bros.).

Fox, A., 'The Retreat, Topsham' in *Proceedings of the Devon Archaeological Society*, Vol. 49, 1991.

Fraser, J. M. & Robinson, B. F., (ed. Sisley, C.), 'Fog Bound' in *The London Magazine*, Aug 1903, (London: Amalgamated Press) [short story].

Fraser, J. M. & Robinson, B. F., (ed. Hutchinson, A.), 'The Trail of the Dead – The Strange Experience of Dr. Robert Harland' in *The Windsor Magazine*, Dec 1902 – May 1903, (London: Ward & Lock) [serialised story in six parts].

French, A., *Ipplepen*, (Exeter: Obelisk Publications, 2003).

Friederichs, H., *The Life of Sir George Newnes, Bart.*, (London: Hodder and Stoughton, 1911).

Gilbert, T., '*A Letter to The Royal College of Physicians of London*', (Unpublished: 17 May 1882) [Thomas Gilbert was the 'Clerk to the University' of Edinburgh and his brief letter reads: "I hereby certify that Mr Arthur Conan Doyle commenced the study of medicine on 1st November 1877 and graduated as M.B. and C.M. of this University on 1st August 1881". This statement is significant in that it contradicts the accepted opinion that ACD commenced his medical studies during Oct 1886. This letter is still held by the library of The Royal College of Physicians: Ref. 'G49 of the ALS (historic letter) collection'].

Goodall, E. W., *William Budd, M.D. Edin., F.R.S. – The Bristol Physician and Epidemiologist*, (London: Arrowsmith, 1936).

*The Granta*, (ed. Lehmann, R. C., Robinson, B. F. & others), 1892-1897, (Cambridge: W. P. Spalding) [these issues include sixteen poems, one song and one playlet by BFR].

Green, R. L., 'Bertram Fletcher Robinson: An Old and Valued Friend – The Adventure of the Two Collaborators' in *Hound and Horse, A Dartmoor Commonplace Book*, ed. Purves, S., (London: The Sherlock Holmes Society of London, 1992).

Green, R. L., 'Conan Doyle and his Cricket' in *The Victorian Cricket Match - The Sherlock Holmes Society of London versus the P.G. Wodehouse Society*, ed. Black, M. C., (London: The Sherlock Holmes Society of London, 2001).

Green, R. L., 'The Hound of the Baskervilles, Part 1' in *The Journal of the Sherlock Holmes Society of London*, Vol. 25, No. 3, 2001, (London: The Sherlock Holmes Society of London).

Green, R. L., 'The Hound of the Baskervilles, Part 2' in *The Journal of the Sherlock Holmes Society of London*, Vol. 25, No. 4, 2002, (London: The Sherlock Holmes Society of London).

Hammond, D., *The Club: Life and Times of Blackheath F.C.*, (London: MacAitch, 1999).

Hands, S. & Webb, P., *The Book of Ashburton – Pictorial History of a Dartmoor Stannary Town*, (Tiverton: Halsgrove House, 2004).

Jackson. K., *George Newnes and the New Journalism in Britain, 1880-1910: Culture and Profit*, (Aldershot: Ashgate, 2001).

James, T., *About Princetown*, (Chudleigh: Orchard Publications, 2002).

Jones, K. I., *The Mythology of The Hound of the Baskervilles*, 2nd Edn, (Penzance: Oakmagic Productions, 1996).

*Kelly's Directory of Devonshire & Cornwall*, 1878, 1879 & 1910, (London: Kelly's Directories Ltd.) [Ipplepen entries: BFR's family and 'Park Hill House'].

*Kelly's Directory of Devonshire & Cornwall*, 1889, 1893 & 1897, (London: Kelly's Directories Ltd.) [Torquay entries: GN and 'Hesketh House'].

*Kelly's Directory of Devonshire & Cornwall*, 1906, (London: Kelly's Directories Ltd.) [Paignton entries: Henry Paul Rabbich and 'The Kraal', St. Andrew's Road, Paignton].

*Kelly's Directory of Devonshire & Cornwall*, 1914, (London: Kelly's Directories Ltd.) [Paignton entries: Henry Paul Rabbich and 'The Kraal', Preston Down Road, Preston, Paignton].

*Kelly's Directory of Devonshire & Cornwall*, 1919, 1923 & 1926, (London: Kelly's Directories Ltd.) [Paignton entries: Henry Paul Rabbich and 'The Kraal', Headland Grove, Preston, Paignton].

*Kelly's Directory of Devonshire & Cornwall*, 1930, (London: Kelly's Directories Ltd.) [Paignton entries: Percy Paul Rabbich and 'Blantyre', Headland Grove, Preston, Paignton].

Klinefelter, W., *Origins of Sherlock Holmes*, (Bloomington, Indiana: Gaslight Publications, 1983).

Lellenberg, J., Stashower, D. & Foley, C., *Arthur Conan Doyle: A Life in Letters*, (London: Harper Press, 2007).

Lethbridge, H. J., *Torquay & Paignton: The Making of a Modern Resort*, (Chichester: Phillimore & Co., 2003) [mentions a number of distinguished visitors to Victorian Torquay, but not GN].

*London and Provincial Medical Directory*, 1848-1869, (London: John Churchill).

*London Medical Directory 1845*, (London: C. Mitchell).

Lycett, A., *Conan Doyle: The Man who created Sherlock Holmes*, (London: Weidenfeld & Nicolson, 2007).

Mann, R., *Buckfast & Buckfastleigh*, (Exeter: Obelisk, 1994).

Marshall, A., *Out and About – Random Reminiscences*, (London: John Murray, 1933).

Marshall, F., (ed.), *Football: The Rugby Union Game*, (London: Cassell & Co. Ltd., 1892) [includes an article by Arthur Budd, the brother of GTB].

Marshall, H. P., (with Jordan, J. P.), *Oxford v. Cambridge: The Story of the University Rugby Match*, (London: Clerke & Cockeran, 1951).

*Mathews' Annual Bristol & Clifton Directory & Almanack*, 1850-1869 (Bristol: Matthew Mathews).

*Mathews' Bristol Directory*, 1870-1879, (Bristol: J. Wright & Co.).

Matson, C. G., 'Automobile Topics: The Paris Automobile Show', *The World*, 11 Dec 1906 [BFR was the editor of this periodical at the time of his death. Various sources report that he contracted typhoid in Dec 1906 during a visit to The Paris Automobile Show].

Matson, C. G., 'Automobile Topics: The Paris Automobile Show', *The World*, 18 Dec 1906.

Matson, C. G., 'Automobile Topics: The Paris Automobile Show', *The World*, 25 Dec 1906.

Maurice, A.B., 'Conan Doyle's The Hound of the Baskervilles', *The Bookman*, May 1902, (New York: Dodd, Mead & Co.).

McClure, M. W., 'Myth-Conception Regarding The Hound of the Baskervilles' in *The Devonshire Chronicle: The Quarterly Journal of The Chester Baskerville Society,* Vol. 1, No. 2, 1989, (Illinois: The Chester Baskerville Society).

McNabb, J., 'The Curious Incident of the Hound on Dartmoor' in *Occasional Papers, No. 1 - Bootmakers of Toronto*, (Toronto: Bootmakers of Toronto, 1984).

*Medical Directory*, 1870-1905, (London: Churchill Livingston).

Michelmore, H. G., 'A letter to the Editor [Noel Vinson]' *The Western Morning News*, 7 Feb 1949 [this letter is dated 2 Feb 1949 and was written in response to comments that were made by J. Dickson Carr in *The Life of Sir Arthur Conan Doyle* about BFR's involvement with *The Hound of the Baskervilles*].

Michelmore, H. G., *Fishing Facts and Fancies*, (Exeter: A. Wheaton & Co., 1946).

Michelmore, H. G., 'Letter to Miss Mary Taylor', (Unpublished: 30 Jan 1907) [this letter records Michelmore's reaction to BFR's death and it is held by the British Library of Political and Economic Science, London: Ref. 'Mill-Taylor, Vol. 29, No. 307'].

Morris, J. E., *Lynton, Lynmouth and the Lorna Doone Country*, (Lynton Urban District Council and the Homeland Trust, n.d.) [gives an account of a journey along the Lynton and Barnstaple Railway].

*The Newtonian*, 1881-1890 (Newton Abbot: G. H. Hearder) [the school magazine of Newton Abbot Proprietary College; it was edited by BFR between 1887 and 1889].

Oswald, N. C., 'The Budds of North Tawton: A Medical Family of the 19th Century' in *Report and Transactions of the Devonshire Association for the Advancement of Science*, Vol. 117, 1985, (Torquay: Devonshire Press).

Paton, N., *Treks in New South Wales*, (Kenthurst, Kangaroo Press, revised edition, 1991) [provides an account of the present day area surrounding Newnes in Australia].

Pearce, D. N., 'The Illness of Dr. George Turnavine Budd and its Influence on the Literary Career of Sir Arthur Conan Doyle' in *Journal of Medical Biography*, Vol. 3, No. 4, Nov 1995, (London: Royal Society of Medicine Press).

Pearson, H., *Conan Doyle, his Life and Art*, (London: Macdonald & James, 1977).

*Pearson's Magazine*, March 1900 – Dec 1904, (London: C. Arthur Pearson Ltd.) [these issues include fifteen articles, two short stories and two poems by BFR].

Pemberton, M., *Sixty Years Ago and After*, (London: Hutchinson & Co., 1936).

Pemberton, M., *Wheels of Anarchy*, (London: Cassell & Co., Ltd., 1908) [novel adapted from notes that were made by BFR].

Pike, J. R., *Torbay's Heritage*: *Torquay*, (Torbay Borough Council, 1994) [mentions a number of distinguished visitors to Victorian Torquay, but not GN].

Pound, R., *The Strand Magazine 1891-1950*, (London: William Heinemann, Ltd., 1966) [this item includes a reproduction of the Manchester Evening News report of 24 Aug 1881 that is said by some to have inspired Newnes to found *Tit-Bits*].

Pugh, B. W., *A Chronology of the Life of Sir Arthur Conan Doyle May 22nd 1859 to July 7th 1930*, (London: MX Publishing Ltd., 2009).

Pugh, B. W. & Spiring, P. R., *Bertram Fletcher Robinson: A Footnote to The Hound of the Baskervilles*, (London: MX Publishing Ltd., 2008).

Pugh, B. W. & Spiring, P. R., *On the Trail of Arthur Conan Doyle: An Illustrated Devon Tour*, (Brighton: Book Guild Ltd., 2008).

Rice, F. A. (comp.), *The Granta and its Contributors 1889-1914*, (London: Constable & Co. Ltd., 1924).

Robinson, B. F. et al. (ed. Hutchinson, A.), 'Chronicles in Cartoon: A Record of our Own Times' in *The Windsor Magazine*, Dec 1905 – Feb 1907, (London: Ward & Lock, 1895-1939) [fifteen illustrated articles about notable individuals who were featured in *Vanity Fair*].

Robinson. B. F., 'How Mr. Denis O' Halloran Transgressed his Code' in *Appleton's Magazine*, Vol. 9, No. 1, Jan 1907, (New York: D. Appleton & Co.) [this was the last short story that BFR wrote].

Robinson. B. F., *John Bull's Store*, (London: Elkin & Co., 1904) [a tax tariff reform anthem; music by Robert Eden (1903) and lyrics by BFR].

Robinson, B. F., 'People Much Talked About in London' in *Munsey's Magazine*, Vol. 37, No. 2, May 1907, (New York: Frank A. Munsey).

Robinson, B. F., (ed. Pemberton, M.), *Rugby Football*, (London: A. D. Innes & Co., 1896).

Robinson, B. F., (ed. Savory, E. W.), *Sporting Pictures*, (London: Cassell & Co. Ltd., 1902).

Robinson, B. F., 'The Chronicles of Addington Peace' in *The Lady's Home Magazine of Fiction*, Aug 1904 – Jan 1905, (London: C. Arthur Pearson Ltd.) [six short stories].

Robinson, B. F., 'The Fortress of the First Britons. A Description of the Fortress of Grimspound on Dartmoor' in *Pearson's Magazine*, Vol. 28, Sep 1904, (London: C. Arthur Pearson Ltd.).

Robinson, B. F., *The Little Loafer*, (London: Elkin & Co., 1904) [a tax tariff reform anthem; music by Robert Eden and lyrics by BFR].

Robinson, J. R., *Fifty Years on Fleet Street* (London: MacMillan & Co., 1904).

Rodin, A. E. & Key, J. D., 'A Plymouth Adventure: Arthur Conan Doyle and George Turnavine Budd' in *Baker Street Miscellanea*, No. 57, 1989, (Chicago, Illinois: The Sciolist Press).

Rodin, A. E. & Key, J. D., *Medical Casebook of Doctor Arthur Conan Doyle*, (Malabar, Florida: Krieger Publishing, 1984).

Ruber, P. A., 'Sir Arthur Conan Doyle & Fletcher Robinson: An Epitaph' in *The Baker Street Gasogene*, Vol. 1, No. 2, 1961, (USA: New York).

Saville, G., 'The War of the Baskervilles', *The Independent*, 11 July 2001.

Selleck, D., *Backalong in Plymouth Town: Stories from West Country History – 1780-1880*, No. 1, (Redruth: Dyllansow Truran, 1984).

Selleck. D., 'Dr. Budd, Bully or Benefactor', *Western Evening Herald*, 21 July 1990 [article about GTB's uncle, Dr. John Wreford Budd].

Selleck, D., 'Tough Talking Cured Patients', *Western Evening Herald*, 16 Aug 1983 [article on GTB's uncle, Dr. John Wreford Budd].

*The Shirburnian*, June 1901 [report about a cricket match played on 3-4 June between Sherborne School and an Incogniti team that featured ACD].

Simpson, A. W. B., 'Shooting Felons: Law, Practice, Official Culture and, Perceptions of Morality' in *Journal of Law and Society*, Vol. 32, No. 2, June 2005, (Oxford: Blackwell Publishing) [a history of convict escapes from HM Prison Dartmoor].

Spiring, P. R. (comp.), *Aside Arthur Conan Doyle: Twenty Original Tales by Bertram Fletcher Robinson*, (London: MX Publishing Ltd., 2009).

Spiring, P. R. (comp.), *Bobbles & Plum: Four Satirical Plays by Bertram Fletcher Robinson and PG Wodehouse*, (London: MX Publishing Ltd., 2009).

Spiring, P. R. (comp.), *Rugby Football during the Nineteenth Century: A Collection of Contemporary Essays about the Game by Bertram Fletcher Robinson*, (London: MX Publishing Ltd., 2009).

Spiring, P. R. (comp.), *The World of Vanity Fair by Bertram Fletcher Robinson*, (London: MX Publishing Ltd., 2009).

Stashower, D., *Teller of Tales: The Life of Arthur Conan Doyle*, (New York: Henry Holt & Co., 1999).

Stashower, D., Lellenberg, J. L. & Foley, C., *Arthur Conan Doyle: A Life in Letters*, (London: Harper Press, 2007).

*Stonehouse Street Directory*, 1852-73, (Plymouth: F. Brendon).

Summers, V., 'The Case of Conan Doyle and the Amazing Dr. Budd', *Devon Life Magazine*, June 1990.

*The Three Towns Directory for Plymouth, Devonport and Stonehouse, 1877*, (Plymouth: W. J. Trythall).

*Torquay Directory and South Devon Journal*, 1 April 1891 – 15 April 1891, [The entries for Hesketh Crescent record that GN and his family were present in Torquay between these dates].

Travis, J., *An Illustrated History of Lynton and Lynmouth 1770-1914*, (Derby: Breedon Books Publishing Co., 1995).

Travis, J., *Lynton and Lynmouth – Glimpses of the Past*, (Derby: The Breedon Books Publishing Co., 1997).

*Vanity Fair* (ed. Robinson, B. F.), May 1904 – Oct 1906, (London: Harmsworth) [these issues include thirty-three short stories, twenty-seven articles, eight playlets, two poems and one song by BFR].

Weller, P. L., 'Deposits in the Vault: Together Again on the Moor?' in *Stimson & Company Gazette*, No. 3, 1992.

Weller, P. L., *The Hound of the Baskervilles – Hunting the Dartmoor Legend*, (Tiverton: Devon Books, 2001).

Wheeler, E., 'Rescuer of Sherlock Holmes', *The Western Morning News*, 24 Oct 1969.

Wheeler, E., 'The Grand Old School of Newton Abbot', *Mid-Devon Advertiser*, 8 Aug 1970.

White, W., *History Gazetteer & Directory of Devonshire, 1850*, (Sheffield: Robert Leader) [entries for Ipplepen].

Will, H., *Ford Park Cemetery, Plymouth – A Heritage Trail*, (Plymouth: Ford Park Cemetery Trust, 2004).

Williams, J. E. H., 'The Reader: Arthur Conan Doyle' in *The Bookman*, April 1902, (London: Hodder & Stoughton).

Wilson, P. W., 'The Lynton and Barnstaple Railway: Interview with Sir George Newnes, Bart.' in *The Railway Magazine*, May 1898.

Zunic, J., 'Origins of the Hound, 1: Bertie and Max', *The Northumberland Gazette*, Nov 1989.

# Internet Sources:

Casey, P., *Clifton Rugby Football Club History*
www.cliftonrfchistory.co.uk

Pugh, B., *The Conan Doyle (Crowborough) Establishment*
www.the-conan-doyle-crowborough-establishment.com

Spiring, P., *BFRonline.BIZ*
www.bfronline.biz

# Reports Prepared for the Authors:

Anon., *George Turnavine Budd*, (Devon Record Office, 2005).
Anon., *Henry Matthews Baskerville,* (Devon Record Office, 2005).
Anon., *Park Hill House in Ipplepen*, (Devon Record Office, 2005).
Anon., *Squire Richard Cabell III*, (Devon Record Office, 2005).
Beckwith, J., *Arthur James Budd*, (The Royal College of Physicians of London, 2006).
Duncan, S., *BFR and The Isthmian Library*, (British Library, 2006).
Duncan, S., *The London Residences of BFR*, (British Library, 2005).
Ferguson, I., *Dr. George Turnavine Budd*, (Edinburgh University, 2007).
Gillies, S., *Articles by-lined by BFR and Published in the Daily Express*, April 1900 – July 1904, (British Library, 2005 – 2006) [a series of seventeen items].
Poole, M., *Henry Paul Rabbich & The Kraal*, (Torquay Library, May 2010).
Willmoth, F., *BFR & Dr. Henry Menzies*, (Jesus College, The University of Cambridge, 2005).

# Private Documents not in the Public Domain:

Anon., *Blackheath Football Club Records, 1875-1898*, (Unpublished: n.d.) [this club was later renamed Blackheath Rugby Club].

Howlett, A., (Unpublished lecture notes: 1976).

McNabb, J., *My Friend, Mr. Fletcher Robinson*, (Unpublished: c. 1985).

Michelmore, H. G., *A letter to Henry Baskerville*, (Unpublished: 8 Feb 1949) [this is a response to a letter from Baskerville, dated 7 Feb 1949, which comments upon BFR's involvement with the *The Hound of the Baskervilles*].

Pugh, B. W., *The Budds of the West Country*, (Unpublished: 2010) [monograph].

Robinson, F., *Reminiscences of Frederick Robinson*, (Unpublished: 1911) [some ten-thousand words of autobiographical notes written by one of BFR's uncles].

Smyllie, F., *History of Meade-King, Robinson & Co. Ltd.*, (Unpublished: n.d.) [extended essay on the development of the company that was founded by BFR's father, Joseph Fletcher Robinson].

Sutton, M., *The Darling Budds of Devon*, (Unpublished: n.d).

# Index

Birmingham, 3, 4, 15, 32, 34, 46.
Black Shuck, 76, 77, 79.
Blackheath Football Club, 27, 29.
Blyton, Enid, 51.
Boltons Boarding House, Torquay, 14.
*Bookman, The*, 79, 92, 96.
Booth, Richard, 73.
Borchgrevink, Carsten Egeberg, 51.
*Bound of the Astorbilts, The*, 93.
Bowden, John, 155.
*Bradshaw's Railway Companion*, 29.
Brigadier Etienne Gerard, 9, 15, 130.
*British Campaign in France and Flanders, The*, 17, 177.
*British Journal of Photography, The*, 4.
*British Medical Journal, The*, 40.
British Museum, 48.
Brook Manor, 131, 134.
Buckingham Palace, London, 15.
Budd, Arthur James (brother of GTB), 27, 31, 32.
Budd, Caroline May (mother of GTB), 27, 31.
Budd, Diana (daughter of GTB), 39, 41.
Budd, Dr George (uncle of GTB), 26.
Budd, Dr George Turnavine (GTB), 3, 4, 22, 25, 26, birth, 27, marriage, 28, BM & CM, 32, death, 39, 104, 107, 112, 114.
Budd, Dr John Wreford (uncle of GTB), 26, 36, 114.
Budd, Dr Samuel (uncle of GTB), 26.
Budd, Dr William (father of GTB), 27, 31, 39.
Budd, Iolanthe (daughter of GTB), 39, 41.
Budd, Kate (daughter of GTB), 39.
Budd, Kate (wife of GTB), 28, 30, 36, 38, 40, 41.
Budd, Margaret (daughter of GTB), 33, 39, 41.
Budd, Mildred (daughter of GTB), 39, 41.
Budd, Nonus (uncle of GTB), 40.
Budd, Robert Sutton (first cousin of GTB), 114.
Budd, William (son of GTB), 39, 112, 114.
Bush Villas, Southsea, 4, 38.

Cabell III, Squire Richard, 84, 134, 137.
Cambridge University, 8, 27, 69.
Campbell, Revd Reginald John, 63, 64, 66, 217, 218.
*Case-Book of Sherlock Holmes, The*, 17, 22.
Casement, Sir Roger, 21.

Zealand tour (1920), 22, American & Canadian tour (1922), 22, American & Canadian tour (1923), 22, South African tour (1928), 23, European Tour (1929), 23, heart attack, 23, death, 23, funeral, 23, memorial service, 24, & GTB, 26, 27, 29, 31, 32, 33, 34, 35, 36, 37, 38, 42, 43, & GN, 46, 48, 50, 61, 66, & BFR, 69, 70, 71, 72, 77, 79, 80, 81, 84, 88, 94, 95, 96, 104, 107, 108, 111, 114, 118, 149, in Torquay, 170, 171, 174, 184, 189, in Topsham 198, 199, in Lynton 63, 208.

*Devil's Foot, The*, 19.
Devon Stag Hounds, 62.
Devonshire Association, 73, 74.
*Dictionary of National Biography*, 47
*Disintegration Machine, The*, 43.
*Does Death End All?*, 3.
Doone Valley, 62.
Dorncliffe, West Street, Ashburton, 141.
Douglas Road, Lewisham, London, 41.
Doyle, Acting Brigadier-General John Francis Innes Hay (brother of ACD), 2, 8, 10, 11, 15, 19, 21, 184, 189, 198.
Doyle, Bryan Mary (sister of ACD), 2.
Doyle, Caroline, Mary Burton (sister of ACD), 2.
Doyle, Catherine (sister of ACD), 2.
Doyle, Charles Altamont (father of ACD), 2, 11.
Doyle, Constance (sister of ACD), 2.
Doyle, Jane (sister of ACD), 2.
Doyle, Mary Helena Monica (sister of ACD), 2.
Doyle, Mary Josephine (mother of ACD), 2, 14, 22, 37.
*Dry Plates on a Wet Moor*, 4.
Duchy Hotel, Princetown, 14, 82, 84, 123, 124, 156.
Durnford Street, East Stonehouse, 33, 34, 36, 37, 38, 41, 105, 107, 108.
Duval, Major Roger Raoul, 70.

East Lyn River, 64.
East Stonehouse, Plymouth, 4, 26, 32.
Edalji, George, 17.
Edinburgh University Medical School, 3, 6, 26, 42.
Edinburgh Wanderers Rugby Football Club, 27, 28, 31.
Egypt, 23.
Elliot Terrace, Plymouth, 22, 35, 37, 38, 102, 104, 111, 114.
Elliot, Colonel James, 104.
Elm Grove, Southsea, 4.
*Erebus*, 51.
*Evening News*, 76.
Exeter & Topsham, 185.
Exeter Hippodrome, 21.

Fawcett, Colonel Percy Harrison, 152.
Feldkirch, Austria, 2.
*Fifty Years on Fleet Street*, 95.

Hesketh House, Hesketh Crescent, Torquay, 53, 54, 178, 180, 181.
Hesketh, Lord & Lady, 180.
Hesketh, Maria (see Palk, Maria).
Hewitt, Thomas, 55, 57, 58.
High Moorland Visitor Centre, Princetown, 120, 123, 127.
Higher Barracks, Exeter, 195, 198, 199.
Higher Luxmore, Higher Leigham, 34, 37, 38.
Hillyard, Mr & Mrs James, 221.
Hillyard, Priscilla (see Newnes, Lady Priscilla).
Hilton, Caroline May (see Budd, Caroline May).
Hindhead, Surrey, 9.
Hingston, Dr C.A., 39.
Hinton Wood, Bournemouth, 221.
*His Last Bow*, 17.
Hoare, Dr Reginald Ratcliffe, 3, 4, 32.
Hobson, Emily (see Robinson, Emily).
Hodder Preparatory School, 2.
Hodder-Williams, John Ernest, 79.
Hollerday House, Lynton, 55, 56, 61, 65, 206, 211, 213, 214, 221.
Holman, John, 56, 213.
Holmes, Sherlock, 3, 4, 6, 7, 14, 15, 33, 46, 75, 80, 95, 97, 108, 118, 123, 130, 134.
Holy Trinity Church, Buckfastleigh, 135, 137.
Honeysuckle Cottage, East Street, Ipplepen, 157.
*Hope*, 3,
*Hound of the Baskervilles, The*, 8, 9, 14, 33, 50, 71, 75, 77, 81, 82, 84, 88, 89, 90, 91, 92, 93, 94, 95, 96, 97, 108, 123, 127, 130, 134, 140, 144, 163.
*How the Brigadier Triumphed in England*, 130.
*How the King Held the Brigadier*, 130.
Hudson, Lawrence, 130.

*Ice Sports*, 95.
*Idler, The*, 47.
Ipplepen, Devon, 68, 73, 82, 84, 96, 155, 156.
*Isthmian Library, The*, 95, 96.

Jerome K. Jerome, 17.
Jesus College, Cambridge University, 69.
Jeune, A.B., 58.
Jeune, Ada Medland, 209.
Jeune, Lady, 57.

Jones, Bob, 55, 57, 61, 63, 64, 213, 217.
Jones, Revd E.H.L., 221.
Jones, Tom, 64 (brother of Bob Jones).

Kelso, Alexander Hamilton (see Hamilton, Alexander Hamilton).
Kemp, C.E., 163.
King Edward VII, 15.
Kipling, Rudyard, 177.
Kraal, The, Headland Grove, Preston, Paignton, 22, 167, 171, 184.

Lady Newnes Bay, 51.
*Lancet, The*, 40.
*Land of Mist, The*, 17, 43.
Langham Hotel, London, 6.
Langman Hospital, Bloemfontein, South Africa, 13, 70.
Leckie, Jean (see Conan Doyle, Lady Jean Lena).
Leckie, Robert (brother of Jean Leckie), 15.
Leckie, Selina (mother of Jean Leckie), 15.
Lee Road, Lynton, 206, 215, 217.
*Leeds Mercury*, 8.
*Liberty*, 7, 23.
*Light*, 21, 184.
*Lippincott's Magazine*, 6.
Little Windlesham, 16.
Littlejohn, William, 19.
London County, 14.
Lord Mildmay of Flete, 149.
*Lost World, The*, 17, 20, 42, 43, 44, 97, 152.
Lucerne, Switzerland, 8.
Lyceum Theatre, London, 15.
Lyndhurst Road, Wavertree, 155.
Lynmouth, 54, 56, 57, 58, 61, 66.
Lynton and Barnstable Railway, 59, 60, 61, 65, 66, 204.
Lynton and Lynmouth Cliff Railway, 57, 58, 65, 66.
Lynton Congregational Church, 63, 64, 66, 215, 217, 218.
Lynton Pier, 65.
Lynton Railway Station, 201.
Lynton Town Hall, 61, 66, 206, 208, 209, 210.
Lynton United Reformed Church (see Lynton Congregational Church).
Lynton, 15, 52, 53, 54, 55, 56, 57, 58, 59, 60, 61, 66, 200.

Newnes, Sir George (GN), 7, 15, 17, 45, 46, as an MP, 52, diabetes, alcoholism, 52, death 52, 55, 213, 221, cliff railway, 57, in Torquay 181, in Lynton 62,64, 208, 210, 213, 219, 222.
Newnes, W. (brother of GN), 221.
Newton Abbot & Ipplepen, 145.
Newton Abbot Railway Station, 146, 149.
Newton Abbot, Devon, 15, 73.
Newton College Proprietary School, 68, 150, 152.
Newton Hall, 152.
*Newtonian, The*, 68, 96.
North Tawton, Devon, 36.
Northcliffe, Lord, 69.
Norway, 7.
*Norwood Builder, The*, 71, 217.
*Novel Magazine, The*, 94.

Oddie, S. Ingleby, 16.
Old Cemetery, The (Lynton), 219.
Old Station House, Lynton, 201, 204, 205.
Olympic Games, 17 (1908), 20 (1916).
Orme, Robert, 193.
Osborne Hotel, Torquay, 53, 179, 180.
Our Society (Crimes Club), 16, 94.

Paddington Station, London, 149
Paget, Sidney, 7, 81.
Paignton & Torquay, 166.
Palk, Maria, 53, 180.
Paris, 1.
Park Hill House, Ipplepen, 149, 153, 155, 156, 159.
Park Hill Lodge, Ipplepen, 156.
Park Street, Clifton, Bristol, 27.
Pavilion Shopping Centre, The (Torquay), 175, 177.
Pavilion, The (Torquay), 20, 22, 174, 177, 184.
Paynter, Joan, 18.
Pearce, Dr David Nigel, 39.
Pearson, Sir Cyril Arthur, 69.
*Pearson's Magazine*, 71, 95.
Peat Cot Hill, 125.
Pemberton, Sir Max, 16, 17, 69, 76, 78, 94.
Pembroke College, Cambridge University, 27.
Penkett Road Beach House, Liscard, 68, 155.

Robinson, Bertram Fletcher (BFR), 8, 13, 14, 16, 26, 48, 49, 51, 67, 72, 218, barrister 69, marriage 96, death 163, grave 163, memorial bench & plaque, 160, 165.
Robinson, Emily (mother of BFR), 68, 143, 155, 163, 164.
Robinson, Gladys Hill (wife of BFR), 96, 97.
Robinson, Joseph Fletcher (father of BFR), 68, 73, 82, 155, 159, 163.
Robinson, Richard (grandfather of BFR), 68.
Robinson, Sir John Richard (uncle of BFR), 8, 95.
Roborough, Devon, 115, 118.
*Rodney Stone*, 9.
*Round the Fire Stories*, 17.
Rowe, Aaron, 82, 83.
Rowe, James, 123.
Royal Links Hotel, Cromer, 14, 76, 79, 80.
Royal Western Yacht Club, Plymouth, 35, 104.
Rugby Football Union, 31.
Russell, Kate (see Budd, Kate).
Russell, William, 130.
Rutherford, Professor William, 3, 42.

*S.S. Briton*, 13, 70, 71, 72, 95.
Savoy Hotel, London, 16.
*Scandal in Bohemia, A*, 7, 50.
Schwensen, Clara Claudia, (sister-in-law of ACD), 11, 19.
*Scorpion*, 36.
Second Boer War, 13, 14, 15, 69.
Selden, 130.
Sherborne, Dorset, 149.
Shireland Hall, Birmingham, 46.
*Sign of Four, The*, 6, 130.
Silcoates School, Yorkshire, 46, 48.
Silvester, William, 88, 130.
Slater, Oscar, 19.
Smith, Elder & Co., 14.
Smith, Herbert Greenhough, 50, 79, 80.
Society for Psychical Research, 184.
South Africa, 13, 70.
South Devon House, Newton Abbot, 149.
South Devon Railway Company, 149, 174.
Southbrook Road, Lewisham, London, 41.
Southsea, Hampshire, 4, 6.
Sparks, Tryphena, 190.

# Further Reading

*The Rise of the Devon
Seaside Resorts,
1750-1900*

by John Travis

ISBN-10: 0 85989 392 8
ISBN-13: 978-0859893923

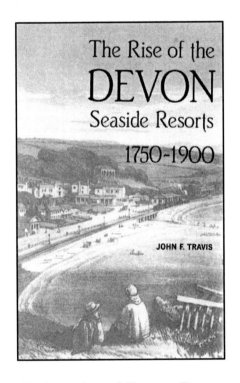

**University of Exeter Press**

Hardcover: 256 pages
(1 Dec 1993).

*An Illustrated History*
*of Lynton and Lynmouth,*
*1770-1914*

by John Travis

ISBN-10: 1 85983 023 4
ISBN-13: 978-1859830239

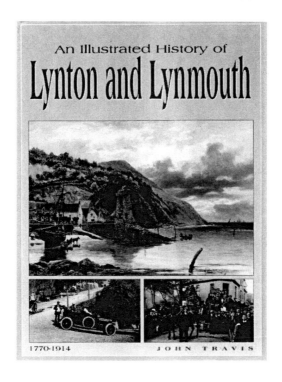

**Breedon Books Publishing Co. Ltd.**

Hardcover: 208 pages
(May 1995).

*Lynton and Lynmouth:*
*Glimpses of the Past*

by John Travis

ISBN-10: 1 85983 086 2
ISBN-13: 978-1859830864

**Breedon Books Publishing Co. Ltd.**

Hardback: 192 pages
(1 Jan 1997).

*Smuggling on the Exmoor Coast,*
*1680-1850*

by John Travis

ISBN-10: 1 899010 60 2
ISBN-13: 978-1899010608

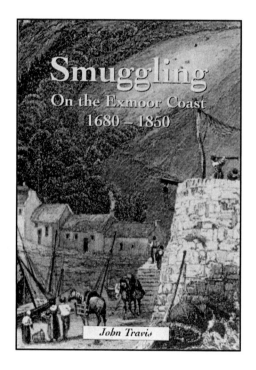

The Exmoor Society

Paperback: 112 pages
(1 Jan 2001).

*Postcards From Topsham*
*Volume One*

by Sadru Bhanji

# Precious Moments (Exeter) Limited

**www.preciousmomentsexeter.co.uk**

*"Written by local historian Sadru Bhanji, Postcards
From Topsham gives an evocative insight into
the lives of people in the ancient town
over the last century."*

***Express & Echo***
(12 May 2009).

*Postcards From Topsham*
*Volume Two*

by Sadru Bhanji

# Precious Moments (Exeter) Limited

## www.preciousmomentsexeter.co.uk

*"...Sadru Bhanji has brought to life the ancient maritime
tradition of Topsham. His Postcards From Topsham
Volume Two gives an insight into the history of
the ancient estuary town near Exeter."*

***Express & Echo***
(31 Dec 2009).

*On the Trail of Arthur Conan Doyle:*
*An Illustrated Devon Tour*

by Brian W. Pugh &
Paul R. Spiring

ISBN-13: 978-1846241987 (English)
ISBN-13: 978-3981132755 (German)
ISBN-13: 978-1904312482 (Spanish)

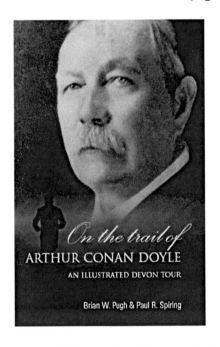

*"Its succinct account of Conan Doyle's association with Devon*
*and with George Turnavine Budd and Bertram Fletcher*
*Robinson is invaluable, and just to follow the*
*Devon Tour on paper is fascinating."*

**The Sherlock Holmes Journal**
(Spring 2008).

*Eliminate the Impossible: An Examination of the*
*World of Sherlock Holmes*
*on Page and Screen*

## by Alistair Duncan

# ISBN-13: 978-1904312314

*"This is a useful reference for Holmes fans and accessible*
*to the casual reader. It has certainly inspired me to*
*read more Sherlock Holmes stories."*

**The Bookbag**
(Feb 2008).

*Bertram Fletcher Robinson:*
*A Footnote to*
*The Hound of the Baskervilles*

by **Brian W. Pugh &**
**Paul R. Spiring**

ISBN-13:  978-1904312406 (Paperback)
ISBN-13:  978-1904312413 (Hardcover)

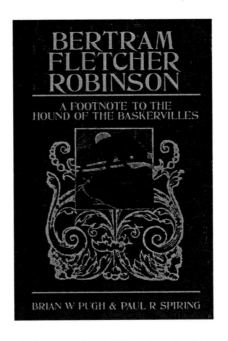

*"A full scale biography of Fletcher Robinson.  Being*
*first in their field allows the authors a virtual*
*blank canvas for their word painting, and*
*this they use to no little effect."*

***The Sherlock Holmes Journal***
(Winter 2008).

*Close to Holmes: A Look at the Connections Between Historical London, Sherlock Holmes and Sir Arthur Conan Doyle*

by **Alistair Duncan**

# ISBN-13: 978-1904312505

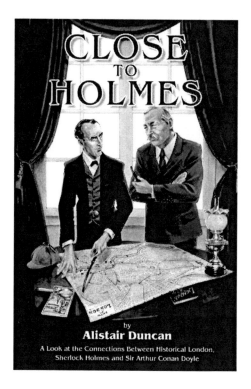

*"Alistair Duncan has visited the significant Sherlockian and Doylean London locations and has shared his enthusiasms in this very readable guide…As an informed and unique addition to further our studies, it is a rare treat!"*

**Sherlock Holmes Society of London Journal**
(Summer 2009).

*Aside Arthur Conan Doyle:*
*Twenty Original Tales*
*by Bertram Fletcher Robinson*

**Compiled by Paul R. Spiring**

ISBN-13: 978-1904312529

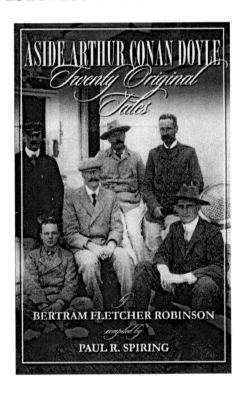

*"The collection proves that Fletcher Robinson was more*
*than capable of producing good work and would*
*probably have gone on to greater things*
*had his life not been cut short."*

**The *Weekend Supplement* of the**
**Western Morning News**
(14 March 2009).

*The World of Vanity Fair*
*by Bertram Fletcher Robinson*

**Compiled by Paul R. Spiring**

# ISBN-13: 978-1904312536

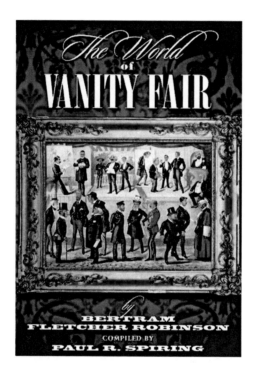

*"Every now and then, you come across a really sumptuous book, where just turning and looking at the pages takes you into another world. Such is the case with this one."*

***The Bookbag***
(May 2009).

*A Chronology of the Life of*
*Sir Arthur Conan Doyle:*
22nd May 1859 to 7th July 1930

by Brian W. Pugh

# ISBN-13: 978-1904312550

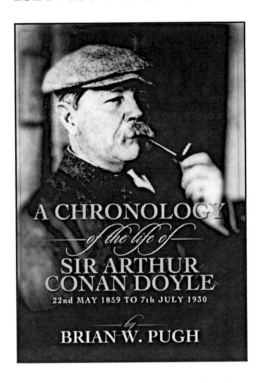

*"There can be little doubt that this book is one of
the most important books on Conan Doyle…
As such it is a truly indispensable
guide for the researcher."*

**Alistair Duncan**
(May 2009).

*Bobbles & Plum: Four Satirical Playlets*
*by Bertram Fletcher Robinson*
*and PG Wodehouse*

**Compiled by Paul R. Spiring**

# ISBN-13: 978-1904312581

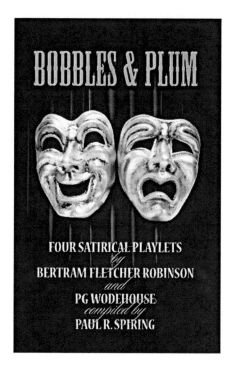

*"The discovery of four satirical 'playlets' by PG Wodehouse,*
*seen by the public for the first time in 100 years*
*this weekend, prove that the humorist – who*
*is often viewed as apolitical – had a strong*
*interest in public affairs from his youth."*

**The Observer**
(26 July 2009).

*The Norwood Author: Arthur Conan Doyle*
*& The Norwood Years (1891 – 1894)*

**by Alistair Duncan**

# ISBN-13: 978-1904312697

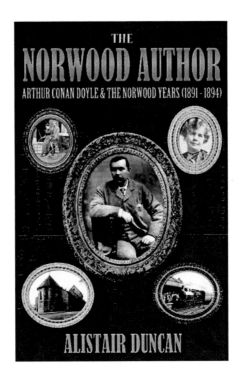

*"Alistair Duncan is one of a distinguished little group*
*whose work takes us just a little closer towards*
*a complete portrait of the man who*
*created Sherlock Holmes."*

**The District Messenger**
(Feb 2010).

*Rugby Football during
the Nineteenth Century*

**Compiled by Paul R. Spiring**

# ISBN-13: 978-1904312871

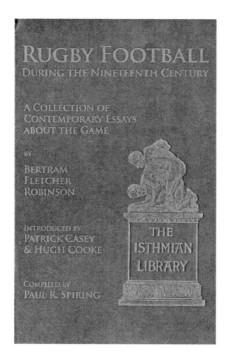

*"There have been some cracking rugby history books
down the years, but never have we been treated
to rugby writing by the men who were there
at the time. Until now."*

**Rugby World Magazine
Book of the Month**
(June 2010).

Lightning Source UK Ltd.
Milton Keynes UK
07 June 2010

155257UK00002B/1/P